Published By
Latin Goddess Press
Winter Springs, FL 32708
http://millytaiden.com
Twice the Growl
Copyright © 2014
by Milly Taiden
Cover: Willsin Rowe

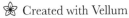 Created with Vellum

TWICE THE GROWL

PARANORMAL DATING AGENCY BOOK 1

NEW YORK TIMES and USA TODAY
BESTSELLING AUTHOR
MILLY TAIDEN

CHAPTER ONE

T alia Barca stared gloomily at her drink. How would she ever survive the next time she saw her ex-husband? The rat bastard.

"So what are you going to do?" her cousin, Nita Islas asked. The soft question broke through Tally's misery.

"I don't know," she muttered and lifted her amaretto sour to her lips. She gripped the cold glass tightly so the shaking of her hand wouldn't cause her to let it drop. Stupid nerves. There was no real reason to be nervous and yet she was. So what that she hadn't seen her ex in years. Her entire family had been invited to her cousin's upcoming wedding, a wedding he'd also attend.

That meant nothing. Okay, it did mean she had to see his dumbass again. To make matters worse, if she didn't attend she'd look like she hadn't gotten over him. How stupid was that when she'd been the one to put in for the divorce in the first place.

"Stop thinking so hard, babe." Nita shrugged her shoulders. Her black, wide-neck top dove to the side and showed off a sparkly bra strap over golden brown skin. "I mean our entire family should know at this point that he was a jerk to you."

"You already know they think it was miscommunication. Makes shit worse that he's been great to most of them. That's why they never really pushed him out of their circle." She swallowed a gulp of her drink, draining what was left in the glass.

"If my parents weren't traveling most of the year they'd support you too. This isn't fair if you ask me. I mean the guy was a dick to you."

A dick with a small dick. That's what she'd called him once she'd given up on trying to make shit work. She sighed. An entire week near Paul of wedding festivities was not what she was looking forward to. He had a god-complex the size of Texas. It made no sense since he didn't have the body or equipment to back that up. Not even something a person should be proud of. He was an all-star asshole.

"I'll think of something." Tally sighed. She'd better think of something ASAP or she'd have to decline attending and that would look even worse. She didn't hide from shit, but Paul was one of those people that the mere thought of him gave her a headache.

Nita slapped her drink on the table with a thump. "What about Mrs. Wilder?"

"Gerri? My neighbor?"

"Yes!" Nita leaned forward. "Didn't she tell you as we were walking out tonight that she's running her business from her apartment in your building?" Nita's brown eyes widened with excitement. "If I recall, she said it's a matchmaking or dating service or something like that."

Tally frowned and swept a long black curl behind her ear, trying to remember the conversation. Mrs. Wilder was her older neighbor from across the hall and a lot of fun. They were the only two on her floor and so Tally visited the older woman quite often. The reason was more so she wouldn't feel alone than Mrs. Wilder being old. Tally didn't really get along with her family thanks to asshole Paul. Now her days were either spent with Nita or Mrs. Wilder. The older neighbor always had a ton of male visitors. She came from a huge family and she'd mentioned some of her grandsons would be moving in to the building in the next few weeks.

"She did say something like that," Tally mused.

"Well, there you go!" Nita passed her empty glass to the waitress, grabbed a fresh one and lifted it to her lips. "Problem solved."

Maybe. Or maybe she'd be in deeper shit if she allowed the elderly woman to mess with her personal life. When it came to men, Tally had some seriously sucky luck. She glanced around the bar that was located a few blocks from her building. The crowd was younger than she cared to be surrounded with, but in a college town, it was bound to happen. At thirty-two, she'd started to feel like a miserable old lady surrounded by hot young men. She didn't see how her personal life could get any better.

"You need to talk to more men," Nita said as if reading her mind.

"I'm too old for dating," she grumbled but smiled at the waitress who'd given her a new drink. "I'm about to get my cat lady starter kit any day now. Men are too much work."

Nita laughed. "You're insane. You're gorgeous! What the heck would possess you to say you're too old? Thirty is young!"

"Thirty-two."

Nita rolled her eyes. "It isn't like you're ninety."

"Sure feels like it," she whispered with the drink by her lips. She winced at how strong it was. Apparently the waitress felt she needed more than her usual dose of liquor. Tally had to agree. She needed a damn miracle.

"All you have to do is stop dating the wrong men," Nita stated matter-of-factly.

She pinned Nita with a glare. "I thought that's what I was already doing. I mean I work at a damn lawyer's office. I don't date any of those assholes. But why is it that when I meet what seems to be a nice, decent man, he turns out to be some kind of double bastard with a side of dickhead?"

Nita's brows curved up. "Wearing a suit to work doesn't mean you should live in one. Cut loose, woman!" She exhaled loudly and pointed a red-tipped fingernail at Tally. "You need to get laid properly."

"Shush!" She glanced around the bar. A couple of the younger guys threw winks in their direction. Flames of embarrassment heated her cheeks. "You're going to get us kicked out of here."

Nita giggled. "What I'd like is to get you hooked up."

"I'd settle for a date."

Nita shook her head. "No. We need drastic measures here. You need to get laid."

"Nita!" She gasped, covering the side of her face with her hand. "Shut up! You make me sound like a desperate cougar."

"Aw come on, Tally. I hate that you have to worry about a date for a family function. You're such a wonderful woman. This isn't something you should be stressing. You should be kicking men out of your door every night."

Right. Because she was such a wild one. Not. With her black-framed glasses, unruly, curly hair, larger than most women curves, and somewhat bitchy personality, she didn't really see herself as a femme fatale.

"I think you've had too many of those drinks."

Tally smiled and patted Nita's hand. "I'll figure something out. I might ask Mrs. Wilder for some help. Who knows? Maybe she can succeed where I haven't."

"I like Mrs. Wilder. I don't care that she can probably chew me into little pieces even at her old age." Nita scrunched her nose. She twirled the small straw in her glass in circles. "It's a good thing she likes you, and therefore me by default, because I have heard some crazy stuff about those shifters."

Tally knew Mrs. Wilder wasn't your regular granny, but she was such a sweetheart. And she was someone she could share her cake addiction with. They took turns baking different things and sharing with each other. It's what fed Tally's chocolate urges and kept her with way too many curves to count.

"Yeah." Tally sucked down a gulp from her new drink. "Who would've thought that I'd become such good friends with a shifter granny."

Nita grinned. "Why wouldn't you? She's sorta bitchy, like you."

"Gee, thanks," she said drily.

"It's a compliment. I'm so tired of these bubbly women that are fake about how they feel.

Feel bitchy? Be bitchy." Nita picked up her glass and pointed to Tally. "This world is filled with too many fake people. You're not trying to be a copy of anyone, Tally. That's why I love you. You're always going to be an original."

Tally grinned. Clinked glasses with Nita and sipped her drink. "Thanks. So far that hasn't really brought anything good into my life."

"It will," Nita assured her. "Go visit Mrs. Wilder and for once tell her you need help. It's not the end of the world to admit to needing a man."

Tally chuckled. "I don't need a man. Not really. I need someone to be my date for the week from hell."

Nita shrugged and motioned the waitress for the check. "Maybe Mrs. Wilder will hook you up." She gasped. "Oh, my gosh! What if she hooks you up with one of those scorching shifters she has visiting her all the time?"

"Now that would be something to celebrate." Tally giggled. "They are so sexy. She told me she has anything from bears, to wolves, to big cats."

"Wow." Nita sighed. "Bears and big cats. I used to have a best friend who was a bear."

"Really? When?"

Nita pursed her lips. "When we lived near the

mountains for dad's job with the fish and wildlife department."

"Was this before you all came back here?"

Nita nodded. "Yeah. We were sophomores in high school. He was so cute with his glasses and almost too innocent face. I told him everything."

"What happened?"

"My family came back here. I loved coming back here after all the years on the road, but that meant my bear friend was left behind. He and I lost touch," Nita said softly.

Tally pulled out one of the many cards Mrs. Wilder had shoved in her hand every time she went over to visit. "Here you go. Why don't you sign up and see what she can get you?"

Nita stared at the clear business card in awe. "Do you really think she can set me up with one of her shifters?"

"Check out the fine print. She's made me read it more than once. She will set you up with whoever she deems to be the right man for you." She read the tiny words on the back of the card and adjusted her glasses. "So, you're pretty much guaranteed a man. I haven't seen a single bad looking one yet."

"You have to do it, Tally." Nita blinked wide

excited eyes at her. "I need to know what she does. You're in need of a date. This really is the perfect solution."

Tally sighed. "At least you're not suggesting those other websites that find your 'perfect' someone."

Nita blinked once. Twice. Then burst into giggles. "I'm sorry. It's not funny after your last episode."

Tally clenched her teeth. She hated that her mother, of all people, had bought her a membership to a dating site that promised to find her soul mate. She swore that every man they sent her way had to have been rejected by every other woman. There was no way that her soul mate was really a forty-five year old man with seven kids, who lived with his mother, had no teeth and worked a maximum of ten hours a week. No way.

———

TALLY STROLLED to her apartment building. Her mind never deviated from thoughts of her dilemma. A date to a family wedding so she wouldn't look like a complete loser in front of her ex. That's what she'd come to. Why did she care so much this time? She didn't know. It might be because she'd been the one rejected by everyone other than her grandmother and Nita. She'd been the one snuffed at functions while Paul, the asshole, had been embraced. She wanted a way to show them that she was doing well. No—she wanted to show she was doing great. Childish? Absolutely, but she didn't care.

Her building in the center of the city was very old. It had the look of something out of the twenties. However, it was well-maintained, with a doorman that had a very slick smile and way too many teeth.

"Good evening, Ms. Barca," Tom, the door man, said. She forced a smile to greet him, her mind still going over her frustrating family.

He sniffed. It was a common thing with a shifter, the sniffing. She wasn't bothered by it. Too many times he'd been the one to give her a heads up of a new perfume that didn't agree with her. So she was more than happy to ignore it.

"Hi, Tom. Have a good night." She dug into her handbag for her keys. The elevator doors opened up ahead. She hated waiting, so she dashed forward to catch it before it closed.

Once she'd gotten inside, she pressed the

button for the top floor where she and Mrs. Wilder lived. The doors were about to close when a hand shot out of nowhere and stopped it.

"We almost missed it," a deep, rumbling voice said. The voice belonged to a big, bulky, tree of a man with shoulder length hair, wearing a black tee, torn jeans and a biker jacket. Hot damn!

"Sorry about that," said the man behind him. Holy wet panties. If the first guy, with his big body and rough, rugged looks made her stare, this one made her mute. Almost as tall as the first guy, which meant they were both over a foot taller than her five feet four inches, this man appeared fresh out of a *GQ* magazine. He wore a white collared shirt with folded sleeves to show his fore-arms, black slacks and a dimpled smile that made his blue eyes sparkle.

"That's...okay," she mumbled.

She forgot all about the elevator and tried to focus on her breathing. The cab was big enough when she was alone, but with those two mountain of men, it felt tiny. Hell, she could feel their body heat closing in on her. And it felt oh so good.

The doors closed. Neither of the men pressed a button. She tried not to gawk, but that was damn hard when the inside of the elevator was mirrors and all she saw was the two gorgeous men wherever she glanced.

She peeked up the biker's body, from his torn jeans, to the bulge in his pants. Crap. That was a big bulge. She slid her gaze up his chest, to the tattoos crawling around his neck, up to his lips. Lips that were currently curled in a sexy grin. When she reached his eyes, she almost melted to the floor. A bright golden color had taken over them.

"Hi, I'm Theron."

I must be dreaming. She gulped. "I'm Tally."

Her attention shifted to tall, blond and sexy. A soft growl sounded from him. She blinked her eyes behind her glasses. Wow. Then it hit her. They were shifters. Both of the men in the elevator with her were also super dangerous. She cleared her throat, her vision not once wavering from blue eyes.

"I'm Connor."

I'm definitely in trouble. She inhaled sharply. "Hi."

She hated that she squeaked the word out, but being that close to those two made her feel all kinds of tiny. Even with her big hips and ass, she did not feel like a very curvy woman. Instead, she felt sort of...small, delicate and... What the fuck was wrong with her?

The elevator dinged on her floor. She scurried out. Not once did she take a look back. Ribbons of fire crept over her cheeks. If those guys had any idea that she'd been fantasizing some very indecent stuff with both of them they would probably stop those sexy smiles. What was her life coming to? She hadn't considered two men sexually at once in...ever! Now she was ready to jump into the arms of a biker and a businessman and beg them to do her every way possible. She opened the door to her apartment and locked herself in. Safety. Her hasty retreat probably made her look like a scared fool, but she really didn't care. If she spent any more time with those two, she might let something inappropriate come out of her mouth. Nita was right. She definitely needed to get laid. Pronto.

CHAPTER TWO

Theron grinned at Connor. They watched the petite and very curvy woman almost trip on her heels trying to get away to the other end of the floor his aunt Geraldine lived at. The scent of her arousal drifted down the hall with the woman. She was flustered but damn was she cute. With her pretty brown eyes, wide behind the black-framed glasses, her long hair in a mass of wild curls and those luscious, pouty lips calling attention, she was way beyond beautiful.

Then there were the curves. In that prim black dress, she'd hidden what he could clearly tell was a gorgeous body. Wide at the hips and narrow at the waist, she was attention-grabbing. Her large breasts and round ass made his cock stand to attention. He licked his lips, savoring the lingering taste of her need.

"I want her," Connor growled softly.

Theron nodded, feeling the same need for the tiny sexy woman. "Me too. We can wish."

Theron didn't bother knocking. He listened to the steps of his aunt closing in on them. A few moments later and the door opened to his favorite person. Four feet eleven, and an absolute fire-cracker, Geraldine "Gerri" Wilder knew exactly how to make any man, no matter how old or tall, feel like a misbehaving kid.

"Get your ass down here and give me a kiss." Gerri slapped his arm. The move didn't sting or hurt, but was her way of getting him to remember she was the adult as far as she was concerned. "You know I can't reach your cheek unless I have the stepstool out."

"Sorry, Aunt Gerri." He chuckled and bent down to kiss his aunt.

Gerri tossed the white chunk of long hair she usually had falling at the side of her face back. The white strands contrasted with the rest of her black hair and gave the older woman an exotic flair.

Gerri harrumphed. "Get your asses inside or I'll have to find that stepstool."

Theron and Connor entered Gerri's apartment and grinned. The scent of fresh baked bread, cake and cookies hit them. They loved when she baked, which was all the time.

"You know I love you, Gerri," Theron began.

"Oh no you don't." She shoved them away from the kitchen toward the dining area. "You'll have to eat dinner before I bring out the sweets. You know the rules."

Gerri didn't care that they were both in their thirties or ready to be the Alpha triad for the Wildwoods Pack. Nope. She only cared that they behaved how she wanted. So they humored her. Besides, both of them loved her to bits.

"How's the mate hunting going?" Gerri asked as they sat down to dinner. The table had been set with large platters of food for the three of them. Being shifters meant large appetites and Gerri accommodated and indulged her nephew and his friend.

The mate hunting was going poorly. With Theron, the Alpha, and Connor, the Omega, being the leaders of the Wildwoods Pack, it made it difficult to find a mate that could be shared between them. Either Theron couldn't find a woman he wanted to help them lead due to her lack of personality, or Connor didn't feel a woman's emotions were in the right place to be their mate.

"It's not going anywhere," Connor replied.

Theron watched his best friend, the one person he shared everything with, including women, sigh in defeat. Their link as Alpha and Omega made them closer than twins, but it also made it difficult to find a woman right for them. Women in the Wildwoods Pack were petty, jealous, and not the kind either would choose to be the third puzzle piece of their Alpha triad. The woman they needed had to be...right. She needed to be open to, not just their relationship, but the link that would ensue between the three. She would be just as Alpha as Theron and just as emotionally empathic as Connor once their bond sealed.

"If you two boys would stop being so hardheaded," Gerri grumbled, passing the mountain of mashed potatoes to Connor. "Then it would be easier for this to happen."

Connor shook his head, his blond hair mussed from running his fingers through it. "She has to be right. A woman on her own. With a personality to match. Someone who won't let the fact that we're who we are intimidate her."

Theron grinned. "And she better be a stunner."

Gerri glared and curled her lip. "Of course, how could we forget that important bit?"

"Hey." Theron chuckled. "She has to agree with both our human and animal sides. That's four degrees of approval."

Gerri's dark brow lifted slowly. "Because you are such a discerning Alpha." Then she turned to Connor. "I know you need to emotionally connect. But him?" She motioned a finger at Theron. "He's a whore."

No. He wasn't. Theron loved women. All shapes and sizes. Although he preferred the short, curvy kind with more than a little to hold on to. He really liked the glasses and long curly hair of Gerri's neighbor. She reminded him of a sexy librarian or schoolteacher. There were also her lips. Christ those pouty lips had given him instant visuals of her mouth on his cock.

"Anyway, we give up," Connor said. "We want you to help us."

Gerri perked up in her seat. She glanced back

and forth between them before speaking. "You're both in agreement with this?"

Not if Theron had his way. But if she could get them someone as sexy as her neighbor, they were all for it.

"Yes, we are," Theron agreed half-heartedly.

Gerri's gaze focused on him. "You will do whatever I say to get you the mate that's right for you?"

He hated having to revert to a dating service, even if it was a paranormal one.

"Yes. I know all about the success of your dating service Aunt Gerri. I don't like having to go through this to get the person that should come to us naturally."

Gerri shrugged, cut her steak and then grinned. "Sometimes you need an extra set of hands." She giggled. "Well, in your case a third set."

His aunt was too much. Connor grinned. Then they were all chuckling.

"Do you need like a list of things from us?" Theron asked. He already knew who he would suggest to her. Even if she wasn't good mate material he'd love to get his hands on his aunt's neighbor. Her scent had driven his wolf to wake and want to play.

Gerri frowned. "Do I look like an amateur?"

Connor's blue eyes widened. "No, but..."

"You will take what I suggest and you won't question me. I know who you two need."

And that's why Gerri was the one handling the Paranormal Dating Agency and they handled the pack.

"If you're sure you don't need anything from us, then we're open to whoever you have in mind," Theron stated for them.

They'd discussed it. Sharing a woman wasn't uncomfortable for them. Due to their connection, it was easier to bond with a third. Though they were not blood related, the animal spirit link between them was so strong, it was almost like they were one entity. Theron was the Alpha that fought and kept people in line. Connor was the emotional rope that united the pack. He took the brunt of the pain, frustrations and turned it all into soothing peace. Together they made the Alpha pair. Once they had their mate they'd be the Alpha triad.

With the meal over, they moved to the living room. That's when Gerri finally let them have cake. Theron didn't even attempt to hide his love for his aunt's baked goods. Gerri was amazing when she baked.

"We should take you to live with us, Aunt Gerri," Theron mumbled between cake bites.

"I don't think so. I have a business to run." She grinned and sat back on her comfy sofa with a smile. "But you are both welcome to visit me whenever you want."

"So..." Connor glanced at him. His worried look told Theron he needed reassurance regarding the mate business. They both knew women in the pack would make life difficult for whatever female they chose if she wasn't part of the Wildwoods Pack.

"Connor, darling." Gerri leaned forward and patted his knee. "Stop stressing so much. The right woman will come for you." She turned to Theron. "I do need to make sure you both will do what I say. It won't be as simple as you might expect. It's not like I'll find your mate in the blink of an eye."

Theron's animal went on alert. He worried that putting their faith on a dating service would be another failure in their search for a mate.

"We understand."

"Alright." Gerri nodded sharply. "Be ready for a possible date soon. It might be a little out of the ordinary, but I think it will work out for you boys."

Theron glanced down at the delicious cake, no longer hungry. Figured that anything to do with a mate would be a new challenge. They hadn't realized how much of a challenge it would be.

When Theron's parents and their third passed in a forest fire, he hadn't fully understood the difficulty of being part of the Alpha triad. He only knew that his parents expected it of him and he would do whatever was necessary to keep the reins on his pack. Even if it meant going outside the pack to find their third.

TALLY HAD ALREADY CHANGED into her pajamas when Mrs. Wilder sent her a text to come for some cake. The scent of the woman's baking had filled Tally's apartment and made her crave sweets like she was looking for a high.

She didn't have to knock, Gerri opened the door before she even got to it. "Hi, Mrs. Wilder."

Gerri rolled her eyes and motioned her into

her apartment. "I've told you that Mrs. Wilder makes me feel old. And I am *not* that old."

Tally grinned at the older woman's pout. She sat down on one of Gerri's pretty beige sofas. The cake was already served and sitting on the coffee table, along with some tea.

"Thank you so much, Gerri." Tally didn't worry about eating sweets late at night. She was too stressed to think about her body. Besides, she was comfortable in her skin, for the most part. Unless really sexy men stared at her the way the two in the elevator had. Like she was a feast and they were starving. That definitely made her wonder if she was missing something when it came to her body. Some kind of image she wasn't aware of. Men didn't usually go out of their way to smile at her like the two had that day.

"You're very welcome." Gerri sat across from her and picked up the notepad next to the cake at her side. "So, I've been thinking about your message."

Tally knew she should have worded it better, but she couldn't. The truth was, she needed help. "The 'I need your help before I look like a loser in front of my family' one?"

Gerri's lips twitched and curved into a full

blown smile. "You won't look like a loser." She waved a blue pen in Tally's direction. "You have me now. I would never allow it."

Tally thought of her ex and her family members. They were all so close. She'd always felt like the outsider in her own family because of Paul. Nita was the only one who knew her side and believed her. Everyone else had been taken in with Paul's slick game. He knew how to work people into believing whatever he wanted. For a while, she'd been one of the people fully invested in him. Then one day, the blinders came off.

"Did you come up with anything?" Tally asked. A sliver of nerves made her hand shake. She hated being so up in the air. She couldn't not go to the damn wedding. Paul had broken her off from the group and made it seem she was the one who had destroyed the relationship with Paul instead of him with his lies.

She had nothing to hide. So why should she be the one not attending. Fuck Paul. And the rest of the family if they felt she was at fault over a relationship too fucked up to work. She'd be damned if she let them push her away. If she didn't go it would be her choice. Not their opinions that would do it.

"I did." Gerri considered her for a long moment.

"Okay..."

"I have some questions for you first." Gerri glanced down at her notebook.

Tally picked up her tea and took a gulp.

"Have you ever had a ménage?"

She choked on the tea she had in her mouth. Gerri passed her a napkin without batting an eye, as if used to that kind of reaction.

"Excuse me?" She coughed.

"Honey, you do know what a ménage is, right?" Gerri's features crinkled in concern.

"Yes, I do. And no, I have never had a ménage."

What the hell did that have to do with getting her a date for a wedding from hell?

"Would you be averse to one?" Gerri shook her head. "Wait, that's wrong."

Thank goodness she'd realized it was wrong to be asking her things like that.

"I mean, would you ever allow yourself to be involved with two men at once?"

She blinked. Her mouth hung open with surprise. She couldn't even find a way to tell her that it wasn't any of her business. Obviously asking the older woman for help had been a bad idea.

"Gerri." She put the cup down, ready to stand. "I really don't think—"

Gerri gave her a look that shut her up. "If there were two men that could give you the most amazing sex of your life, would you do it?"

Well, when she put it like that.

"Um." She bit her lip. "Together?"

"Yes, together."

"Are they going to do stuff to each other or only to me?"

Gerri gave a tired sigh. "No, darling. It's all about you."

"Hey, I don't know much about this stuff or how it works," she said, a little irritated that Gerri looked at her like she was a woman having sex for the first time. She'd had sex, dammit. She hadn't had any amazing sex. She'd had lots of crappy sex for sure.

"I'm sorry, Tally. I don't mean to put you on the defensive. There are ménages that involve men and women all getting involved with each other. I want to know your preferences."

"I wouldn't be averse to trying. I mean, I'm not a damn virgin but I'm not stuck in the old ages either. I'm not the most adventurous woman out there," she admitted. "Two good-looking men? Giving me great sex? That is kind of a no-brainer."

Gerri chuckled. "Smart woman."

She leaned forward, trying to see what the hell was on the notepad. "What does this have to do with my date?"

"Nothing. Merely curious." She shrugged. "We have so many handsome men in my system. Care to describe how you like yours? Are you more into businessmen with kind eyes and wicked smiles or do you prefer hot bikers with tattoos and ass-hugging jeans?"

"Shit. If I could get those two rolled into one, I would be the happiest woman in the world." She sighed.

Gerri had described the two men from earlier. The image of the two men pleasing her in all kinds of ways sent her temperature skyrocketing.

"Got someone in mind already?" Gerri's eyes went wide for the first time. "You do!"

She shook her head in denial, heat crowding her cheeks. "I remembered your guests from earlier. Those guys were sinfully sexy."

A slow, predatory grin slid over Gerri's lips.

"My nephew and his friend. Yes, they are very handsome boys."

More like hot as hell with a side of scorching, but handsome worked too.

"How's your luck been with men?" Gerri asked.

She didn't bother lying. "The pits. All I meet are jerks or rejects from the weirdest date club."

"Really? But you're such a pretty girl," Gerri mused.

"Come on, Gerri." She twisted her lips into an unhappy smile. "I know I'm not bad looking, but my hair is too curly, I have too many curves and my attitude apparently needs some sweetening was what my last two dates told me." She clenched her teeth hard. "They also said I shouldn't have such high expectations because looks aren't everything," she grumbled, folding her arms over her chest. "This because I mentioned to one guy that his profile photo was not him."

"Oh?" Interest sounded in Gerri's voice.

"He used a photo of a very good-looking man. A man he looked nothing like." She frowned, growing angry all over again over that episode. "Apparently the photo was of a British

31

actor. My date said he was always told he looked like that actor so he didn't see the need to post his own photo when that would do."

"But he doesn't look like the actor?"

She bit her lip to keep from growling. "No. The actor had hair. My date didn't. The actor was fit. My date looked like a slob. His sweats had stains on them. And..." She scrunched her nose. "He had really yellow teeth."

"Wow," Gerri said. "That sounds like a terrible date."

"It gets worse." She glanced down at her plate covered with smudges of icing. "He took me to have coffee and I ended up having to pay for him because he 'forgot' his wallet."

"Oh, you poor girl." Gerri gasped, horror visible over her features.

"I have at least one hundred other stories like that. Dating sucks and I won't do it anymore. But I need someone to come to my family wedding and I want the man to be the hottest you can find. Even if I never see him again," she said hopefully. "I want everyone to shut their mouths about my dating life already. So, can you help?"

Gerri nodded. "Yes, I believe I can."

"The hotter the man, the better. I want tongues to wag."

Gerri's giggles filled the apartment. "My dear, you are most definitely my kind of client. I have exactly what you need."

"Good." She stood. "I'll need him for my first event, the bridal shower, in a week. Have him show up at the restaurant. I don't have time to come home. I have a long day and we'll have to meet there." She headed for the door with Gerri by her side. "I trust your instinct. So whoever you pick for this I'm okay with."

Gerri grinned. "I'm glad. You'll have an open mind though, right?"

She had the biggest open mind. Shit. She was letting an elderly friend find her a man for a wedding. If that wasn't crazy she didn't know what was.

"Yes, I'll have an open mind." She stopped at the door. "Make sure he has hair, nice teeth and clean clothes. Other than that, I can probably let everything else slide."

"Can do," Gerri promised. "Don't worry. Your dream date will come true."

She laughed. "I'll settle for a nice guy. One who won't expect me to put up with body odor."

"Trust me, nothing like that here."

She nodded and waved as she headed for her side of the floor. "Good night, Gerri."

"Good night, Tally. Have faith. It will all work out."

Easier said than done.

CHAPTER THREE

Tally growled and honked. Again. She was so late. Her date had probably left already. Not that there was any way she could have known her asshole boss would hand her a stack of calls to make right when she headed for the door.

"Bastard." Lawyers sucked hairy balls.

Rush hour traffic only added to her frustration, but she pushed it away. Gerri had called her and said that she would be pleasantly surprised by her date. Tally's excitement grew once again. Though a bridal shower was far from her idea of a perfect date, she wanted to make a certain 'I could give two fucks what you think' impression with her family. Hopefully whatever hot man Gerri had chosen would help her do the job.

She swiped clammy hands over the skirt of her strapless blue maxi dress. She wasn't usually into strapless, but it was pretty and she really liked how the dress fit.

Nita had instigated her into buying it. Telling her that it made her look sensual and sexy. She'd spent years ignoring her own sex appeal and hiding her curves because she was, according to her family, fat. She wouldn't do that anymore. Her body was hers and if she wanted to strip to nothing and wiggle her ass for her new date, then she'd do exactly that. Right after she had a few drinks. Liquid courage was her best friend.

The restaurant the family had chosen for the bridal shower was an expensive one. That meant that everyone had to look the part. Air tripped in her chest. She'd forgotten to tell Gerri to make sure the man was dressed appropriately. She would not freak. Would not freak.

Dammit, she was freaking. What if the guy showed up in shorts and a tank top?

"Oh, lord." She slammed her hand on the steering wheel as she turned the corner to enter the parking lot of the restaurant.

Her brain had decided that was what would happen. Her date would be inappropriately dressed and she'd still end up looking like a fool. Not what she needed.

She hopped out of the car. Forget demure and composed, she rushed into the entrance of the hotel and ran down to the private party room. She stepped on a wet spot on the floor and skidded down the hall.

Bam!

She slammed into a huge body that appeared out of nowhere. Massive hands curled around her arms to hold her steady. She glanced up and lost her breath.

"Hello, beautiful Tally," said the blond guy she'd met at the elevator in her building.

Before she got a chance to find her voice, hot guy number two from the elevator made an appearance. She'd walked into the Twilight Zone.

"Oh, god," she mumbled.

"She's got a great voice," biker guy said. Wait. She remembered his name. Theron. And blondie was Connor.

"What are...what are you two doing here?" she asked. There was no stopping the awe in her voice over how amazing the two men looked in a suit. Her mouth watered. In regular clothes the men were scorching enough to melt panties, but in suits, they gave new meaning to panty-dropping sexy.

"We," said Theron as he moved around to her side. "Are your dates for the next few days."

She gasped. No way. Gerri couldn't be that evil. "I think you must be mistaken."

Connor smiled, the grin turned his movie star good looks to orgasm-inducing sinful. "We are your dates, Tally. Would you reject us?"

"I don't need two dates," she stated more to herself than them. She really didn't need two sexy men eyeing her like she was the hottest woman in the world. Did she?

Theron lowered his head. "We're a pair," he whispered by her ear, his breath tickling the side of her face.

She bit back a moan and squeezed the clutch in her left hand in a death grip.

Someone turned the corner at that moment. It was Paul with his new girlfriend. She really did have the worst luck.

"Talia?" Paul said, glancing back and forth between Tally and her escorts. "I'm surprised to see you here."

His tone said he expected her to bow out because he was there. Not in this lifetime jerk-wad.

"Oh? Why's that? I did tell Roland and Susan I was coming." She forced herself to smile. Anger heated her blood. She wanted to lash out and punch the high and mighty smirk off his face.

"Who are your companions?" Paul asked, shoving the slim blonde woman forward. "This is Candy."

"Nice to meet you." The blonde smiled. She was friendly where Paul gave them a snobby smirk.

Tally glanced up at the two men on either side of her. What could she say?

"I'm Theron and this is Connor," Theron introduced them for her.

"Are you co-workers of Tally?" Paul asked, much too interested.

"No," Theron answered before Tally got a chance to. "We want a lot more than professional things out of her. She's ours."

"Excuse me?" Paul lost the smile. It was almost worth it that Theron made her sound like a hooker who they'd bought, if only to see the surprise on Paul's face. "Are you saying you're sleeping with her?"

"Paul!" the blonde admonished.

"I really don't see how that's any of your business," Tally spit out.

Theron grinned down at Tally, curling his hand around her wrist. She bit her lip, holding back the urge to shudder. Then, to make things worse, he drew circles with his thumb over her skittering pulse. Meanwhile, Connor slid his fingers over the back of her neck.

For a moment she forgot all about Paul and focused on the sensation of the two men caressing her.

"Tally is much too special just for sex," Connor said, pinning her with his gaze.

Theron lifted her hand up to his lips and kissed over her erratic pulse. "That's right. We're interested in the long-term of having her. She's the only woman who can make us whole."

Lust pooled at her core. Fire shot from her nipples down to her clit. If she could get the two guys alone at that moment, all bets were off. To say things that perfect to her ex without her even asking them to meant Theron and Connor were ideal for what she needed.

"Aw," said Candy, breaking the intimate moment between Tally, Connor and Theron. "You guys are so cute. Why don't you say things like that to me, Paul?"

Tally cleared her throat. Her mind was a whirlwind of erotic images where Theron and Connor were doing some pretty dirty things to her. And she was begging for more.

"Well," Paul said in a clipped voice. "We'll see you inside."

He entered the private party room and left them behind without another word.

"Jesus, you guys are good." Tally's mind reeled. They were both still caressing her and they were now alone. The sensual smiles did some things to her lungs she couldn't explain. It was like she'd lost the ability to breathe normally. "You can stop now."

Theron chuckled. The sound made the hairs on her arms stand on end. It was deep, rich and so sexy her girl bits quivered with need.

"Why would we want to do that?" Connor asked, voice low and rough. His light touch drove her closer to forgetting what she was there for and focusing more on what she wanted to go do.

"Um..." What was the question? "Didn't

Gerri explain to you guys I only need to pretend to be dating to get my family to see I am not a total loser and they can kiss my ass?"

"I'd prefer it if you allowed me the privilege instead," Theron said softly.

She blinked and met his gaze. "What privilege?"

"The one of kissing your delectable ass."

Wow.

She moved away from them, her mind a total mess of wants and needs. "Hang on a second. I didn't really expect two escorts tonight. I don't really know what to do with two of you. And you don't have to act like I'm the hottest woman in the world when nobody's around."

"But you are the hottest woman to us," Theron stated and Connor nodded.

They closed the distance around her. She didn't want to want them, but she did. Both men pulled at some deep primal urge inside her. It was like a whole new part of her was being exposed and she wasn't sure what to do with it.

"We'll make it good for you," Connor said as if reading her mind.

Oh, she had no doubt about that.

Theron cupped her cheek. "No, we'll make it fucking amazing for you."

Jesus H. Christ!

"All you have to do is give us a chance." Connor smoothed his hands around the curve of her ass.

Her pussy ached with how turned on she was. "A chance at what?"

"Being ours."

"We need to go inside," she murmured. Only half her brain reminded her that they were one door away from chaos and she needed to control her hormones.

CONNOR WATCHED Tally from across the room. Theron handed him a glass of champagne.

"What do you think?" Theron asked.

Connor knew what Theron wanted to know. Was she emotionally stable and strong enough to be part of their Alpha triad? She was. Though there was a lot of sadness and one very fiery attitude in her, Tally was perfect for them. He knew it from the warmth that hit him to the bone when he touched her. Theron had the same feeling. It was one of the things he could sense from their connection.

"She's perfect. In every way." He didn't bother to hide how much he wanted her himself. "If she can accept us, our triad would be complete."

Unlike a lot of packs. Wildwoods Alphas came connected to an Omega. Theron and Connor had known from birth they'd be a triad. It was normal. For years they'd shared women, but never a mate. This was new ground. Choosing a human mate made things even more difficult. There was the question of what if her body didn't take the change? What if she was challenged for her position?

"The females could be trouble. Especially Keya. She's been angry about our rejection for a while now," Theron said. They glanced at each other and then back at Tally. She appeared deep in conversation with an old woman. Every few moments she'd laugh or smile. That was their sign she didn't need any intervening.

"Yes, but we'd have to treat her like one of our own and let her handle it how she sees fit."

Theron handed a passing waiter his empty champagne flute then folded his arms over his chest. "Up to a point. No way I'd let anyone hurt her. She's so tiny. And Keya comes from a former Alpha family. She might not be Alpha in our group, but it's in her blood. She wants to lead. I won't let anything happen to Tally."

"She's a lot stronger than she seems, Theron. Very fierce." Connor homed in on the tripping heartbeat that belonged to Tally. She was aroused. A second later, she glanced up and met his gaze. Oh, yeah. She wanted a taste. She might not know how deep things truly were, but for now, they'd take her sexual attraction to them and use it to encourage her to be with them.

"Could take a while to get her on board with our needs," Theron grumbled.

"Then we need to use whatever means necessary to make her see our side of things." Connor grinned at Tally. She licked her lips and skittered her gaze away from them.

"I think I like where this is going." Theron chuckled. "This will be fun."

"I'll start it off," Connor offered and readied to march to Tally.

"Keep your eyes on the prize," Theron growled low.

Their prize was sweet Tally and her sexy body

all for them. For a mate. Connor strode to Tally to do whatever necessary to break down her walls. A handful of steps and he was there.

Connor tapped her on the shoulder. Her skin was so smooth, softer than anything he'd ever touched. And the color was driving him to distraction. A smooth caramel that put his paleness to shame.

She glanced at him, her eyes wide behind her glasses. He loved how innocent she appeared before lust filled her dark brown eyes.

"Would you like to dance?" He offered his hand and watched her stare at it for a mute moment.

"Go on, girlie," the older woman said. "He's handsome and you look amazing in that dress. Ignore all the idiots and have a good time."

"Thanks, Grandma Kate."

"Don't worry, if I see Nita I will tell her you are looking for her." The old lady grinned.

Connor pulled her into his arms on the dance floor, already packed with a bunch of couples. The music was soft, so there was no need for outrageous dance moves that might get someone hurt.

Tally glanced everywhere but him. He sensed

the tension in her muscles. Her arousal was what brought a smile to his lips.

He leaned down, pressing their bodies tight together and murmured by her ear, "You need to relax, Tally."

She inhaled sharply. Her ragged breaths and almost inaudible moan made his cock jerk. He slid a hand down her back to the curve of her and pressed her into him. He wanted her body cradling his cock.

"Oh, my..." she whispered.

"That's all you, beautiful." He brushed his lips over her shoulder. "I'm so hard I can't think straight."

She reeled back, staring at him wide-eyed. "But—but I haven't done anything."

He smiled at her shocked expression. "You're doing enough by smelling so delicious and looking so appetizing."

He guided her to a darkened corner where he could press her closer to him and torture himself with her softness.

"Connor, you're both really handsome men, but I have never..." She glanced around. "This isn't the same room."

He'd pushed her through an open curtain to

an empty side room. "I wanted to be alone with you."

She blinked and licked her lips.

"Christ, Tally. If you keep doing that I won't be responsible for my actions."

Her wet pink tongue swooped over her bottom lip again. "Doing what?"

He pressed her back against a wall. "That. Licking your lips and reeling me in to do the same. I have to taste you."

Her mouth opened on a gasp and he used it as his first opportunity to kiss her. Their lips touched and instant fire spread through his veins. She moaned in the back of her throat. The sound was soft and so damn sexy he gripped her waist harder than he intended. He ached to be inside her, feeling her pussy stretch around his cock. The moment she curled her tongue over his, all reality ceased to exist. She was the only thing his wolf and Connor focused on.

She raked her nails up his arms. She squeezed him hard over the material of his jacket. With each grasp, she added a husky little moan that drove him wild. She wiggled her hips closer. She was wet. So wet. He could tell from the thick perfume drifting from her.

He pulled away from the heaven of her lips to kiss down her jaw.

"Tell me you want this." He bit down on her bare shoulder.

"Oh, god," she moaned.

"Tell me you want us both. Tell me you'll try." He pressed kisses down to her breasts. He wanted so badly to push the material down and suck on her nipples. To lick and lave and bite her into coming.

"I..."

He rocked his cock into her. His hard and throbbing length got no relief. Desire twined knots in his spine, down to his balls.

He cupped her breasts over her dress, squeezing her tits and licking at her exposed flesh. Her moans dug deep into him. They pushed him to continue the dangerous seduction. She gripped his jacket and pulled, until their lips were once again feasting on each other.

Her boldness only made the animal inside him hungry. She slid a hand down and cupped his cock. Her small grip tightened fast. He groaned, loving the feel of her on him even if over his pants. She might be pressed between him and the wall, but she was the one controlling things.

Then, the sound of footsteps closing the distance jerked him out of his sexual haze. He blinked and curled an arm around her, darting straight for the door to the outdoor section of the restaurant.

The moment might be gone, but he knew her fire only needed some fanning. She was definitely the one for them. It was time to wear down her defenses and get her to come to them willingly.

CHAPTER FOUR

Tally blinked past the sexual haze and tried to remember what the hell had happened but she couldn't. She'd been at a bridal shower for her family. Then she'd been making out with Connor. After that they'd driven her home and now she was sitting in their car wondering what the hell was going on.

She climbed out of the vehicle on unsteady legs. As if he read her mind, Theron was there. He gave her an arm to lean on and she bet, if necessary, he'd have carried her to her door. How she knew that? She had no idea. But her instinct when it came to Theron and Connor was like a radar pointing straight to heaven.

When they got to her apartment, she couldn't

think of anything to say. She ached and her body throbbed with unfulfilled need.

She met Theron's sexy dark gaze. "I—"

"We won't push if you aren't ready," he said.

Connor stood just a step to her right.

Theron bent down and cupped her face. Their lips were mere inches from each other and by god did she want to get a taste of him too. "We don't have to go if you ask us to stay."

She gulped. Her legs shook at the implication. Both of them. Pleasuring her. Solely focused on whatever it was she wanted and making it a reality. She wasn't sure if she was nervous, excited or scared over the prospect. No man had ever given her great sex. Despite their amazing good looks and sexy talk, she didn't know how they'd rate in bed.

"Try it," Theron encouraged. "I'll lick your pussy until you can't move."

She leaned back against her half-open door, her grip tight on the handle. Theron caressed her face, down her neck to her breast. He didn't touch her aching nipple. Not even to taunt her. He bypassed it and she almost growled in anger. She was so turned on that minimal touches could get her to explode.

Connor took that moment to move in on her. He pushed forward, caging her between the two. "If you allow us, you'll get enough pleasure tonight to last you a lifetime."

She groaned. Christ why did he have to say shit like that?

"But if you give more time with us a chance, you'll get a lot more than you ever imagined."

Dear God. How could he say things like that and expect her to run inside and say good-bye? Screw wondering. Nita was right. She needed to get laid.

She glanced from one to the other and nodded. "Come inside."

The moment the words left her lips, both men took over so fast she wasn't sure what happened. One second she was at the door, the next she was in the middle of her living room with Theron kissing her, his hands cupping her face and Connor pressing his cock against her back, his hands squeezing her breasts.

Clothes flew off. Theron growled against her lips. His tongue darted between her lips and dominated hers. It was like a battle of wills. She didn't know how long she could last, giving him back suck for suck, lick for lick. Not when all she knew was need. Desire. The urge to beg him to make her come.

Connor tugged her dress down her body along with her panties. Air puckered her nipples tight. Then his hands were there. On her skin. Tweaking her nipples and sliding down to cup her pussy.

"Fuck, Tally," Connor groaned. "You're wet. So wet."

He spread her pussy open, one finger pressed right at the heart of her pleasure.

She moaned, her body rushing to the peak she wasn't ready for. Theron continued to make love to her mouth. His tongue swiped in and out, thrusting and retreating with the same rhythm of a man fucking a woman.

Theron kissed down her jaw. He fluttered kisses down to her breast. She gasped as a roll of heat shot down her body. He sucked her nipple into his hot mouth and grazed his teeth over her flesh. She bit her lip, her mind lost in the sensation of pleasure from his tweaking one nipple and sucking the other, to Connor moving his hands to mold her ass.

"You're so beautiful," Connor whispered by

her ear. His words were low, rough, with a bite of growl that only made her wetter.

Theron pushed her tits together, moving back and forth from one to the other. He licked, he sucked, he bit and she gasped for air. Her leg muscles gave out on her, but Connor was there. He held her by the waist and pressed his lips down her spine.

"I got you. You like having us touching you, Tally?" he asked.

She blinked, trying to get a good view in the dimly lit room. Her brain had stopped working and all thoughts focused on how quickly she was readying to burn from the inside.

"I do. I like it...a lot," she admitted.

She'd never have thought herself this adventurous. Somehow, the boring administrative assistant had taken a leap into the pool of the daring. With one man caressing her from behind and the other licking his way down her front, she'd turned into a risk taker and she was damned if ever she went back.

"Tell me what else you like," Connor asked, his breath stroked her lower back.

"I want to be touched," she stated, digging her nails into Theron's arms for support. Breaths rushed in and out of her lungs. Each lick from Theron's lips on her nipples seared a desire to be possessed by the two men.

"How?" Connor tapped her to spread her legs wide. Then he spread her ass cheeks and slid his tongue down her crack. Her breath hitched with each swipe of his tongue around her hole. An instant trembling took hold of her legs, but Theron held her up with his strong hands.

She slid her hands into Theron's long hair and raked her nails over his scalp.

"Oh, my God!"

Theron's mouth left her achy nipple with a wet pop. She glanced down to meet his bright golden gaze.

"You smell fucking delicious." His voice, pure churned gravel, turned her already tight nipples into hard little points.

She yanked him up by his hair. The brightness in his eyes increased and a low rumble sounded from his throat.

"Take your clothes off," she ordered.

He grinned. It was a sensual delight for her to watch him slowly remove his jacket and the rest of his clothes. Connor had moved down, to lick up and down the back of her thighs to her pussy and back to her ass.

She lifted her hands to her breasts. Theron's nostrils flared. She pulled and pinched at her nipples.

His pants dropped to the floor. He had to be one of the most beautiful men she'd ever seen. Body covered in tattoos, nipples pierced and an erection so impressive she wanted to drop to her knees and suck him.

"You like what you see?" His words were flirtatious, sexy.

"I do. Do you?" She squeezed her breasts, cupped them and silently offered the large mounds to him for his pleasure.

"Baby, I more than like what I see. You've got me so hard." He gripped his shaft in his hand and stroked up and down in a bold move. "I can't wait to fuck you."

He leaned forward, took one of her nipples into his mouth and bit down. She gasped. The combination of him biting her and Connor now shoving his tongue up and down between her pussy lips turned her legs to jelly.

She blinked and Theron was gone. His move took place so fast she didn't realize for a few seconds his lips weren't on her. The scuffling of moving furniture sounded. He grabbed her from behind and tugged. She fell on one of the sofa chairs, with Connor still between her legs. Theron came around the chair, his cock level with her face.

She glanced up and licked her lips. "Come closer. You want me to taste you?"

"I want to see your pretty lips wrapped around my dick," Theron said, his voice rougher than before.

Connor turned, he pushed her legs over the armrests of the sofa and rubbed his face on her pussy.

"You taste like the sweetest dessert," he groaned between her legs.

She leaned back, pushed her ass closer to the chair's edge and turned her head to face Theron. She gripped her hand around his cock, stroking him from root to tip.

She met his gaze as she touched him. His jaw clenched. Heat emanated from his body in powerful waves. "Is it hard for you to let me touch you?"

"Yes," he groaned.

She opened her lips, licked a slow circle

around the head of his cock and glanced at him again. "Why?"

"Because..." He moaned as she took a lick from his balls up to the crown of his shaft and flicked her tongue in circles. "I want to be deep inside you. Feeling your wet hot pussy gripping my dick in a tight hold."

She spread saliva with her tongue over his cock. Theron slid his fingers into her hair, grabbed chunks of it and pushed his dick into her mouth.

"Suck it."

CHAPTER FIVE

Connor shoved a finger into her pussy, the dual intrusion pushed at the arousal coursing through her body. She moaned, took more of Theron's large cock into her mouth and wiggled over Connor's mouth.

Connor licked and laved her pussy. She was already soaked with her own cream. He pressed his tongue over her clit. He retreated and drove back in. Passion burned bright at her core.

Theron thrust in and out of her mouth. Slowly at first, but then with more power and speed. She rubbed the underside of his cock with her tongue. Every plunge into her mouth sent fireworks to her clit. Her jaw burned from how wide she had to hold her mouth open, but Connor's continued sucking of her pussy took her mind off any discomfort.

"Fuck, baby," Theron growled. "You have such a wet little mouth."

She jerked him with one hand in conjunction with her sucks. He was hard and smooth as silk. She slid her other hand down to grip Connor's blond hair and pressed him closer to her pussy.

"That's right, princess," Theron groaned, moving in and out of her mouth. "Show him how you like to get fucked."

Her belly quivered. Theron gripped her hair tighter with one hand and fondled one of her breasts with the other. Connor moved his fingers out of her pussy. They were replaced with his tongue. He fucked her, lapped at her juices and growled. At first it was soft, but each little growl built the anticipation twisting knots in her core.

Then his licks turned faster. Harder. Rougher.

He turned relentlessly with speed and agility. She gasped. It was hard to keep up with sucking on Theron's cock when she was ready to come. Her muscles tightened.

Theron pulled his cock out of her mouth and leaned down to kiss her. He drove his tongue into her mouth and rubbed it over hers. This time she was there with him. Desire unlocked something inside her she didn't know existed. A thirst for more. A need for a deeper sexual enjoyment. Something she'd never had with any other man.

The tension at her core reached a limit. Connor sucked her clit into his mouth. And growled. Pleasure blasted through her body in a wave that caught her off guard.

She choked out a scream, digging her nails into Connor's scalp, holding him between her legs. Her body shook as the wave crested. She barely breathed. He continued to lick and suck her through multiple mini-orgasms. It was unlike anything she'd ever experienced before.

Gasps and quick breaths were the only sounds in the room. That and a low rumble from Theron.

He cupped her face in his hands and brought his own mere inches from hers. "I want to fuck you so bad I can't think straight."

She glanced down at Connor, who licked her scent off his lips. "What about you?"

Connor grinned. "Don't worry, beautiful. I know how to wait my turn."

She didn't get a chance to say more. Theron lifted her in his arms, then sat on the sofa she'd been sitting on and slowly lowered her body on to his. She pushed forward, biting her lip as the head of his cock speared her pussy.

"Oh, fuck!" Theron growled. "You're a tight little thing."

Little? There wasn't a little thing about her. She moaned at the almost burning sensation of his cock pressing into her pussy walls. He was big and long and thick. All wonderful things except that she hadn't had sex for a while and most of the men she'd been with didn't have his length or girth.

She met Connor's gaze, watched him strip and then sit on a chair from the dining room, directly in front of them. He was fully erect and ready.

Theron pressed her down on his dick, hard. She groaned at how filled she felt. He was in her fully, so deep she could barely breathe.

"That's fucking perfect," he groaned. He lifted and dropped her on his cock. She didn't need further urging. She rocked on his lap, not really lifting but rubbing her insides with his dick in an incredible way.

"Oh, my..."

Theron grabbed chunks of her hair and

pulled her back. He licked the back of her neck and cupped her breast with his free hand. "I like how wet you are. So slick and tight."

She gulped, her gaze still locked on Connor. Connor jerked his cock. A bead of liquid dripped from the slit of his dick. He spread his palm over it and continued to stroke. A new ball of tension started to twine inside Tally.

Theron rocked his hips under her, urging her to move faster. "Ride me, baby."

His words, so rough and low with that hint of need, pushed her arousal higher.

Connor continued to touch himself, his beautiful tanned ab muscles contracted with every up and down motion he did. His breath sounded ragged. Or maybe that was hers. She couldn't be sure what she was hearing anymore. Her own heartbeats sounded louder than anything else.

Theron grabbed her hips. He lifted and rammed her hard on his cock. Each slide down woke nerve endings she didn't even know existed. Her body was a giant time bomb waiting to explode.

Connor licked his lips, his eyes glowing with his animal power. "You are so fucking sexy," he groaned. "I love watching your tits bounce while he fucks you."

Her pussy clenched around Theron's cock. It was so erotic to hear him say that.

"I can see your clit peeking between your pussy lips," Connor said. "Want me to lick it?"

He really loved oral, but it made her want to do something for him instead. "Why don't you come over here so I can help you out with that?"

He stood, stalking his way to her. She was still bouncing on Theron's cock when he stopped in front of her. Connor roped her hair around his hand and she leaned forward to take his cock into her mouth.

Connor groaned. She suctioned her cheeks tight, allowing him deep into the back of her throat with ease. His size wasn't as imposing as Theron's so it was easier to suck him off.

"God, you have such perfect lips," Connor groaned.

"She's got a perfect pussy too," Theron rumbled from behind her.

Somehow, she was able to ride Theron and suck Connor without losing her rhythm. She jerked Connor with one hand while she sucked. His cock was smooth. Almost like hot velvet in her mouth. Meanwhile Theron's bigger dick rubbed her insides like no other man's ever had.

Connor started to thrust in and out of her mouth with more speed. Theron's body turned tight under her. He sat up, curled a hand around her clit and fingered her hard little nerve bundle.

"I want you to come with me," Theron growled. "I want to feel your pussy sucking my dick and drinking my cum."

Her nipples ached with how badly she wanted to come. The things he said were more images to add to the erotic arsenal assaulting her brain. Connor's body tensed as well.

Theron rammed her down hard. Once. Twice. He pinched her pussy and she pulled Connor's cock out of her mouth to scream.

A new, much more intense orgasm rocked her. Her pussy gripped tight on Theron's cock. He did one more deep painful thrust and roared. His cock grew, pulsed and filled her with his cum. She was knocked into a second powerful orgasm from the feel of his cock almost vibrating inside her.

She jerked Connor, he clenched his jaw and threw his head back. Her instinct took over. She leaned forward as his semen spurted out of his cock. Loud growls sounded from Connor. His cum landed on her breasts and slowly slid down her chest and nipples.

He groaned with each continued jerk until his cock was semi-hard but spent. She leaned back into Theron's body. He was still deep inside her. She lifted her hands to rub her breasts and massage the cum over her tits.

Connor groaned while watching her. "You have no idea how much I like that."

She licked her lips. "I liked you coming on me more."

Her night of a seemingly simple bridal shower date had turned into unbelievable sex. She didn't want to think too much or she'd start finding all kinds of flaws with the past few hours.

Connor helped her off Theron and lifted her in his arms. She allowed him to at that point. Her legs were still shaking and she didn't want to fall on her face.

"Which way is the bedroom?" Connor asked, the sexy grin back on his lips.

She directed him and glanced over her shoulder as Theron followed close behind.

TALLY WOKE to the smell of food. Her stomach grumbled. She turned on her side and blinked her eyes open when memories of the previous night rushed through her brain.

Oh. God. She'd had sex with two men. Two incredible hot and very skilled men. She sat up in a rush. Her bedroom was a mess from when she'd jumped in the shower with Connor, only to have Theron state she had to have a shower with him too. Towels littered the floor and clothes were thrown all over.

"What did I do?" She gasped.

She jumped out of bed and tossed clothes out of her way to find her purple fuzzy robe. Spotting a hair tie, she twisted the long, curly and very messy mass into a bun on top of her head. Then she rushed to the bathroom and washed her face and brushed her teeth. Finally, she found her glasses on the dresser and put them on.

Nope. She was not going to look at her reflection or she would surely have a mild panic attack.

Loud laughter and the smell of coffee urged her to the kitchen. Theron sat in a pair of sweats and no shirt at her kitchen table with a plate of food. Connor sat next to him in boxers and a tank top with a cup of coffee in front of him.

To make it all even better, Gerri sat there with them. Smiling.

"Hi?"

"Come over here, darling." Theron slapped his lap and motioned her forward.

Blood heated in her face. She'd never been overtly sexual with men like she had the previous night, so this was new territory.

"Sweetheart, you need a better robe," Gerri said, her gaze taking a deep dive down to the material that dragged behind Tally.

"Thanks, but I like this one." She strolled forward, almost tripping.

"Well, it clearly doesn't like you." Gerri shrugged. "Come eat. I made enough food for everyone."

Tally's dining room table, which was seldom used, was covered with plates of food. From scrambled eggs, bacon, sausage, pancakes, to fruit and pastries. It was like a restaurant had moved into her apartment.

She bypassed Theron's lap and sat on the fourth and empty seat at the table. She opened her mouth but no words came out. Really, what could she say to Gerri? That she was angry at her for sending her two of the hottest men she'd ever met? Men that had given her more orgasms in one night than those she'd given herself throughout her thirty-two years? Instead, she went for the coffee and prepared herself a mug.

"Are you okay?" Connor asked. His worried frown appeased her fears somewhat.

"Yes, I'm fine," she lied.

Connor, Theron and Gerri glanced back and forth at each other.

"You are most definitely not fine," Gerri stated. "You are clearly having an emotional dilemma."

She would not, could not, talk about that with them. No way in hell.

"Connor," Theron said, taking the attention off her. "Maybe if we explain our way a little, Tally would understand some."

Gerri stood. "I'll go back and do dishes. You all talk."

She wanted to listen to them, but she also felt she had to address Gerri. Didn't look like she'd get the chance now.

"Do you prefer to speak to us together or one on one?" Connor asked, reading the turmoil inside her. He was clearly perceptive and she had a difficult time as it was talking to them at the same time.

The men glanced back and forth at each other and Theron stood. "I'm going to take a shower." He leaned over the table and kissed her. "I'll be back shortly, beautiful."

CONNOR WATCHED indecision flash through Tally's eyes. He smelled her confusion over the new situation between them. As Omega, his first instinct was to calm her down. As a man who wanted her for a mate, he needed to make sure she was comfortable with how things worked for their pack.

"I need to understand what it is you two want," she said, voice low. There was a slight tremble to it that kicked him hard in the gut.

"You know we are shifters," he stated, more to verify what she already knew.

She sipped the cup of coffee and glanced at him, her gaze direct. "Yes, but I didn't realize you all shared women."

"Not all packs do. Things vary from one to the next. For Wildwoods, sharing a mate is custom and part of the norm. It's a way of life." He grasped her hand on the table. "Other packs share a single mate among multiple pack members. We've come across the single couple packs. Nothing is taboo in the shifter world."

Questions lit in the depth of her gaze. "What do you mean nothing is taboo?"

He shrugged. "When the heat strikes, couples could have sex anywhere. People shift and don't have clothes, it's natural to walk around naked."

Her eyes widened and her mouth turned into a perfect pouty O. "Walk around naked?"

He grinned. She probably didn't realize it, but when he'd said people have sex anywhere, her cheeks had turned a dark crimson and she'd licked her lips.

"Yes. Sex is natural. So is nudity. We're very sexual creatures." If she was going to be part of the pack, she needed to know what she would be getting into.

"So you..." She cleared her throat. "You and Theron, you want me?"

"Yes." God, how they wanted her.

For the first time ever, the men and the animals were in sync. She'd been the answer they needed. They wanted her for a mate. And there would be no turning back.

"For how long?" She scrunched her nose. "You want me as a lover, shared between the two of you for a while?" She pushed her cup to the side and pursed her lips. "So if one of you gets tired of me, does the other one get me? Or do you both pretty much just go with mutual votes?"

CHAPTER SIX

"Don't do that." He shook his head. "That's not how we are."

She leaned forward on the table, the scent of her distress mingled with anger. A new light of hostility sparked in her eyes. "I'm sorry but I just don't see how a relationship of being lovers could work long-term."

That was the main problem with non-shifter mates. They didn't get the different way of life. "We are born and raised this way."

He knew he wasn't getting through to her, so he stood and marched around the table. He offered her his hand and watched her stare at it for a second. She took it. He moved to her long sofa and pulled her on his lap. She struggled for a moment, but once she saw he wasn't letting her go, she stopped and sighed in defeat. He shifted her so her back was leaning on the armrest and he could look at her face.

"What is the one thing you've always wanted in a mate?"

"A partner? I guess someone who is honest and can love me for me and not for who he feels I should be."

"Think of us as the first men that will give you that." He pushed a stray curl behind her ear. She blinked with curiosity behind her glasses.

"What do you mean give me that?" She glanced down at his mouth.

He wanted so bad to stop the conversation and kiss her. She had the most beautiful pouty lips and he'd never tire of watching her slide her tiny pink tongue over them.

"When we search for a mate, it has to be someone who is perfect for us on multiple levels. Mainly we have to be attracted to her in our human bodies. Your scent has to attract the animal inside."

She raised her brows in obvious shock. "Wait, you and Theron had to want me and so did your...eh, wolves?"

He nodded. "We hadn't had luck until you. We love a woman with curves. That is just our preference. You're gorgeous. I wouldn't dare compare you to anyone else because nobody else has made me want her as much as you. No other female has made Theron and I agree she is the one meant to fit as our third and make us whole."

"I...I don't know what to say," she mumbled. "There's so many women out there that have a lot more experience with two men."

"Oh, darling." He brushed his lips over hers, not able to contain himself any longer. "You are the one. No matter what any other woman has, you have given our connection the emotional boost it needs for Theron to lead and for me to engage the pack. You're who we need. Something about you is perfect for us."

"Connor, this all sounds so nice, but what happens when you tire of me?" She sounded sad.

"That won't happen."

"What do you mean? It happened with my ex-husband and a host of ex-boyfriends. I have bad luck with men."

"A mate is for life. There are no others once one is found. Only one mate for our pair."

"You mean to tell me that without knowing

me at all, but based purely on instinct and scent, you two feel I'm right to spend the rest of your lives with?" The disbelief was obvious in her tone.

"Yes." He didn't bother denying it.

"Connor, come on. I'm a pretty modern person, but taking on a relationship with two men, something I've never done, is scary enough. Added to that you want this to be something committed? I don't know if you know this, but we just met. This is crazy."

"Give us a chance, Tally." He glanced deep into the fear he saw in her eyes and tried to soothe the tumultuous emotions in her heart. She was a strong woman, but fear could make her choose the path they didn't want for her.

"I have to think."

"I have an idea," Theron said, entering the room as she finished her sentence. He was freshly dressed and appeared unperturbed by her words. He gave Connor an open mental link to allow him to see his thoughts.

Connor's fears for Tally dissipated somewhat. Theron's idea was sound. If they could pull it off, then she wouldn't have the worries in her mind.

"What's your idea?" Tally turned to Theron.

"We date." He grinned. "It's what humans do,

right? Date to get to know if someone is mate material?"

She nodded. "They do, but wait, so this means the whole mate thing is off the table?"

"No!" he and Theron said at once.

"It means you need to be reassured and we are happy to do whatever is necessary for you. You're our priority now. We want you to be happy and comfortable or we won't be," Theron replied.

"Well." She frowned. "I still have this wedding to go to. I guess that's as good a place to start as any. But that's not until next weekend."

"How about we start with something simple," Theron suggested. "Come with me for a walk."

Connor nodded when she glanced at him. "Go for it. I think spending time one on one first and then as a group could really help you see how much this can work."

"Are you sure? Won't that mess with the idea of being a..."She gulped. "A triad?"

Theron grinned. "Not even a little. Connor and I know each other well enough to know neither would ever try to push the other one out of the way. What we want is unity."

"I'll shower and change in your guest room," Connor offered. He sensed she needed the time to be alone, to think about what they offered and to decide what she wanted. "We'll go and give you some time to yourself. Tomorrow, Theron can come and take you for that walk if you're in agreement."

The last thing they needed was for her to feel like she was being pushed into anything. They wanted her ready, willing and able to be the woman for them. Though they already knew she was the one, she still had to come to that conclusion. No amount of pushing or pressure on their part would encourage her trust. That would come with time.

THERON GLANCED AT TALLY. She wore a long, sexy dress that hugged her curves like a second skin. It wasn't tight, it draped perfectly over her large breasts, small waist and abundant hips. His mouth watered the moment he saw her.

She'd worn her hair in a ponytail that drove him crazy. He loved her curls and wanted to see them hanging loose down her back. She pushed a long strand behind her ear and adjusted her glasses. The prim, schoolteacher look had never been such a turn-on.

How was it possible that she did that to him? She was so unaware of her beauty. It would probably kill him if she continued to bite and lick her bottom lip for much longer. She hadn't said anything of his holding her hand the entire time they'd been walking through the massive park. He'd deliberately brought her to one that bordered his land. It was silly, but thinking of her that close to his home brought a smile to his lips. If only he could do something to alleviate the confusion he sensed in her.

"What is it that concerns you about a relationship with us?" he asked.

She sighed loudly. They went a few steps more before she finally answered. "I've been married to the jerk you met a few days ago. I've dated so many men that only wanted to sleep with me or to find a woman to take care of them." She stopped and turned to him. "Frankly, I'm sick of it. I'm not doing it anymore."

"You shouldn't have to. A partner should be someone who takes what you already have and makes it better. Someone who makes you happy to have them in your life."

Her sad smile broke his heart. "That's what we'd like to think. And that's what men always advertise. I'm not sure I'm the right woman for you two. I'm too bitter."

"You're not bitter. You have just had some very bad experiences and I understand your hesitation." He cupped her cheek and stared deep into her troubled eyes. "All I can ask is for you to give us a chance. No pressure. If at any point you feel the need to go or that this isn't working, we understand," he lied. They'd probably die without their third, but he wouldn't tell her that. She didn't need to be pushed. She needed coaxing.

She pursed her lips and turned back to strolling. "When I was a kid, I swore my parents had the most amazing marriage ever. I mean really awesome. They were always hugging and smiling and laughing. I wanted that for me." She chuckled. The sound came out a pained laugh. "Then I grew up. I heard the yelling behind closed doors. I saw the bruises she tried to hide. I questioned her and do you know what she said to me?"

Waves of her pain surrounded them. He had a hard time yanking back the animal who wanted to offer her comfort. He bit back the growl threatening to escape and pulled her closer to his side. "What did she say?"

"She said that cheating comes natural to everyone. That it was my responsibility to accept it and let it go. That if I wanted a marriage to work I would have to understand my place as a woman." She shook her head. "I don't buy that for a second. I refuse to believe it and I won't settle for it."

"So she feels it's okay to have a relationship with a partner that isn't committed to being with only one person?"

She nodded. "It gets better. She said the only way she's stayed married this long is by having affairs herself. All her time away with family and friends allowed her the ability to meet up with men and do her own thing."

His chest ached with the bitterness spilling from her lips. She hurt badly and he didn't know how to stop it. "You have to understand not everyone thinks that way."

She shrugged. "I know. I've met other couples who don't have that as part of their lives. But the truth is, I have bad luck with men." She veered off the main park path and crossed to a desolate hill with a thick grassy patch. She stopped, glanced down at the view of the forest and sat down. "I have awful luck with men. Hell, I have terrible luck in general. You both don't need my bad luck in your lives."

"Let us be the judge of what we need. All we want from you is a chance."

She gazed out in the distance. "I have no experience with shifters other than Gerri. And she's a handful."

He grinned at the sound of her soft laugh. "That she is. She has been like a mother to me and Connor."

Tally folded her legs under her and turned to him. "How do you do it?"

He saw interest and curiosity spark in her eyes. "Do what?"

"How do you share a woman and not worry that she will fall in love with one over the other or more than the other?"

That was tough. "In an ideal world, you'd fall in love with both of us. We want you to have the emotional link with both of us to create a strong bond."

She nodded slowly but said nothing.

The breeze swirled strands of her hair forward. He leaned close and placed the strand sticking to her lips behind her ear. Her eyes widened behind her glasses. Then, to tantalize and drive him completely crazy, the scent of her arousal drifted into his lungs. Her heartbeat accelerated under his touch. Her skin heated and she licked her lips.

"I hope you understand." He moved closer, pushing her to lean back on the grass, until her back hit the ground.

"Understand?" Her voice quivered.

"I can't stop myself." He stared at her mouth and allowed the hunger he felt inside to show itself a bit in his features.

Her eyes widened and she gasped.

"I can't control my need to feel your body under me," he said and leaned over her. He groaned as he lay between her legs, his cock nestled over her pussy. "You are so soft, Tally."

She gulped. "Theron, I don't think—"

"That's right, darling. Don't think. Just go with your instinct." He leaned down and crushed their mouths together. She tasted divine. Like the sweetest honey and ripest fruit. Her body cradled him with her softness. He almost came on the spot at the first swipe of her tongue over his. No longer tentative with her touches, she thrust into his mouth and moaned. The sound was sexy as hell. For every groan, she moaned. For every thrust, she curled her tongue over his. He pulled at the hem of her skirt, pushing it up her thigh. He needed to feel her smooth skin under his palms.

She yanked her face sideways, whimpering, "Oh, Theron. Christ that feels good."

His cock jerked in his jeans. There was little he could do to stop the thrusting between her legs. She spread her legs wider and glanced into his eyes. "Do it. Now. Here."

Normally he wouldn't let himself get carried away this way. But her eyes, dark with desire, and her lips, swollen with his kisses, had his wolf pushing at the skin. Everything inside him shifted into pleasure mode. It was all about getting her off right now.

He kissed a path down her neck, to the neckline of her dress. With a single tug, her bra popped above the dress. The sheer lace holding her breasts showed off her puckered brown nipples.

She wiggled under him, the heat of her core driving his cock to painful hardness.

"Please..." she moaned a husky little plea that

sent shudders down his back. She probably didn't realize how much she affected them. At that moment, all he wanted was to please her. To see her smile and watch her body unravel when pleasure hit.

He sucked a nipple into his mouth over the lacy bra, using the material to add a new dimension of torture to his woman.

"Oh, God!" She slapped her hands on his biceps. Her hips rocked into him. The sensation drew a groan from his dry throat. She was so responsive. To even the smallest touch. She'd gasp or mewl or moan. So softly. So desperately that he could think of nothing but shoving his cock so deep into her he'd watch her eyes roll to the back of her head and scream as she came.

He bit down on her nipple at the same time she scored her nails hard on his arms. Her eyes were closed and her mouth puffed air in and out of her pink lips.

They'd wanted a mate for so long. One who would please them physically and emotionally. Though she was emotionally scared, she was so fucking perfect in every way for them. Her body turned him on like no other woman had before. It might be her hidden sex appeal. She didn't need to flaunt it. Her inner light shone through the fear.

He peeled back the bra and sucked her tit into his mouth. Her gasp and immediate shudder pushed the animal forward. He had a hard time controlling the beast. He liked her scent. Liked her taste.

He licked back and forth between her breasts, sucking, nipping and repeating.

"Theron...I don't think I can take much more of this." She met his gaze. Her passion-dazed eyes broke the limit on his control.

He slipped his hand between her legs and found her wet center. Christ, she was soaked and dripping heat. He ached to be inside her, to feel her pussy clutching at his cock with every slide into her velvety walls. Spreading her lips open, he slid a finger around her clit. She curved her back, pushed her pussy into his hand and groaned.

"More. Give me more, please."

He loved the sound of desperation in her voice. Her muscles shook with how tense she was. He slowly fingered around her clit, tapping the tiny hard bundle lightly before moving away. He knew she was close and wanted to make it really good for her.

"Oh, baby you are so fucking wet. Do you know how badly I want to be inside you?"

She raked her nails up his arms and into his hair to tug his mouth back on her nipple.

"Suck me. Make me come," she ordered.

God, she was so sexy when she got all dominant and aggressive. He knew that wasn't something she did often. He sensed her normal hesitation deserting her. He sucked her plump breast and bit down on her nipple. At the same time, he slid two fingers into her slick pussy and fucked her so slow he knew she'd probably yell at him soon.

"You...are...evil," she moaned. "I am going to shatter if you don't hurry."

"Oh, no. You're exactly where I want you, beautiful." He licked the valley of her breasts and nibbled on the other nipple. "I want you so desperate that when you come, your juices flow over my hand."

Her chest quaked with how hard she breathed. He blew air over her nipples. They scrunched up into tighter little points.

He quickened his moves, thrusting in and out of her pussy with first two, then three fingers. He prayed that his erection wouldn't turn into blue balls because this was not going to be one of those times where he'd get to slide up into her sleek wet pussy and get to feel her contract around him like a velvet glove.

Her breaths panted out of her in low moans. He watched her face, her features concentrated fully on reaching the peak. He bit down on her nipple and tapped her clit hard. She choked out a moan. Her grip on his hair loosened as did her body under him. She went soft and a low gasp sounded from her.

She glanced at him and smiled. Not a half smile, either. It was a smile of someone having been pleasured to the point she couldn't stop the grin.

"I have never done anything like that in a public park," she said, blinking the sexual clouds out of her eyes.

"It doesn't matter where we are, Tally." He swiped his tongue over her nipple one more time before fixing her dress. "Your pleasure is my priority."

He stood, ignoring his aching hard-on and helped her to her feet. "Are you good to walk?"

She nodded but glanced down at his cock. "Are you good to stay that way?"

He grinned. "This wouldn't be my first time going home with no relief. I can handle it." He cupped her face and kissed her softly. "I wanted this to be for you. I'm perfectly fine as I am."

He wasn't really fine, but fuck, he wouldn't make her feel like she had to suck his cock in the middle of a public park either. He wanted her to have this moment. It wasn't about him needing her to return the favor.

"Are you sure?" she asked and glanced around as if trying to decide what to do next.

"Baby, this was all about you. I am happy to wait." He met her gaze. "For you, I'll wait as long as I have to."

CHAPTER SEVEN

Tally took Connor's hand. He leaned down into the vehicle to help her out. The front of the banquet hall was filled with expensive cars. Her cousin's wedding had finally arrived. They'd gotten to the church in time to sit in the back row and watch quietly. No one had noticed them or paid them any mind. Exactly how Tally liked it. The reception would be another story. She'd been dating Connor and Theron for a week now and things were a lot better than even she anticipated.

"You're going to have to come out of the car, darling," Connor taunted. She'd voiced her opinion on how unexcited she was about the entire event, but her call with Nita and then her grandmother had sealed the deal. She'd go and show her face. Show everyone she was alive and well with two hot men by her side.

"I'm coming," she grumbled. The wind whipped her curls all over her face. She'd forgone the glasses for a set of contacts.

"I really hate that you didn't wear the glasses today," Theron said, coming around the car to her side. "I have a thing for the prim school-teacher look."

She had no idea what he was talking about. Tally might not be overtly sexual with displaying herself, but she didn't try to hide her body either. She wore what she liked. That was usually long, soft dresses. For the wedding, she'd decided to wear a shorter dress that hugged her curves. Connor had complimented her on it at least five times in the past hour.

"Have I told you how beautiful you look in that dress?" He winked.

Make that six times in the past hour.

"I don't think so, no." She grinned. "I may never get out of this dress if you keep it up."

She allowed them to lead her into the reception hall. They'd deliberately taken their time so that things were busy by the time they arrived.

The reception was being held locally in a large banquet hall. A massive party location known for hosting top-notch events.

She found their names and seating assignments on a table at the entrance to the main hall. Inside, music pumped over large speakers. Disco lights blinked in different colors and a DJ urged the crowd to do the electric slide.

"I'll go get us some drinks," Theron offered when they reached their table.

The crowd cheered as the music ended. A new slow song started and the DJ called couples to the floor.

Connor squeezed her hand. "Come on, let's dance."

"I don't know..." She stumbled to her feet and followed behind him.

"You want to dance. Stop worrying over what others will think."

He was right. She did want to dance. That was one of her favorite songs the DJ was playing. Connor held her close, staring deep into her eyes.

He lowered his face close, until his lips were by her ear. "Ignore the people."

She laughed. She was the one that usually said that. When had things changed? And more importantly, did she really care what anyone thought? Not really. She smiled and let her muscles relax. Until that moment, she hadn't noticed how stiffly she held herself.

"That's my girl."

Their dance and fun time was short-lived. Someone bumped into them from the right. She opened her mouth to apologize but stopped at the sight of Paul and Candy.

"You came?" Paul asked, his face a mask of disgust.

"Of course I came. This is my family." She stopped dancing to face him.

"Have you even bothered to think of what it's doing to them for their friends to see you waltzing around with two men like—"

"I'd be very careful of the words that come out of your mouth," Connor whispered, his voice hard.

Paul glared at him and then back at her. "You have no shame at all, do you?"

"I don't see why you're worried over my personal life. You're not part of my family." She curled her hands into fists. Connor stood behind her, he'd tried to gently get her to move to his side, but she didn't budge. This was her fight and she was going to handle it all by herself.

She saw Theron from the corner of her eye, ready to move forward. She met his gaze for a second and shook her head.

Grandma Kate stopped dancing with her uncle and joined them.

"What is going on? Why aren't you all dancing?"

Nita moved to Tally's side. She had waved at her cousin when she'd walked in, but hadn't spoken to her yet.

"What's the problem here?" Nita asked, her voice held more than a little aggravation. "Why did you stop them from dancing, Paul?"

Paul gave Nita a murderous look. "I'm genuinely disturbed for the family."

Nita and Tally's gazes met. Nita rolled her eyes and Tally sighed.

"Why are you disturbed, Paul? I see no reason to be worried," Grandma Kate said.

"With all due respect, Kate, your grand-daughter is making a spectacle of herself with these two men she's brought to the wedding." He huffed.

Connor let loose a soft growl and Paul took a step back.

"Why are her dates any of your concern?"

"I'm worried for you, madam," he stated. "I would not like to see your good name and that of your family spoken of poorly due to Tally's sexual deviance."

"My what!" Tally screeched. She'd kill him. The jerk had actually had the guts to talk shit about her in the middle of a packed dance floor.

"You heard me!" Paul threw back loudly. The music stopped and everyone listened to the argument. "You're sleeping around from one guy to another but that's not enough for you, is it? You have to bring them to a family event. To show the rest of polite society what kind of life you lead."

Tally lifted a hand to slap him, but Connor was quicker. He grabbed her arms and pulled her back. "He's not worth it."

"Let her hit me," Paul instigated. "I'll have her arrested for assault."

"You asshole!" Nita hissed. "You think we'd take you over Tally?"

Paul turned to Grandma Kate. "I'm sorry to say this, but your granddaughter is a whore!"

The crowd gasped. Grandma Kate took a step

closer to Paul, raised her sixty-five year old hand and slapped him so hard it resonated around the hall.

"You listen and you listen to me well," Kate said softly. "This is my family. Talia is my grand-daughter. You're nothing. Get out of here before I find my cane and shove it up your uptight ass."

Paul's wide eyes and shocked face was one look Tally would never forget.

"I—"

"Get out!" Kate yelled. "I'm too old to put up with crap. Others might have let your assholery slide, but I won't. I don't want to see your face at any other family functions, or believe me, my cane will find a new home up your ass." She turned to Tally's uncle. "Get him out of here."

Tally's uncle nodded. "Whatever you say, mom."

Connor released Tally. She started to move away from the dance floor when her grandmother stopped her.

"Talia, come here, please."

Tally turned back to Grandma Kate and stopped next to her. Kate grabbed Tally's hand in her own and glanced around the hall. "This is my granddaughter. She'd had a poor excuse for parents, but she's got me."

"She's got us too," Theron yelled.

"And me," Nita added.

Kate nodded. "So if anyone here says anything about my Tally, they'll be seeing a side of me anyone rarely sees. She's not alone."

Tally's eyes filled with tears. She never needed anyone to protect her or stand up for her. But there she was, surrounded by her grandmother, Connor and Theron and Nita, all showing her how truly special she was.

"Put the music back," Kate said to the DJ. "We're not done dancing over here."

TALLY GIGGLED AGAIN. "Theron if you keep pressing that same spot I'm not going to stop squirming."

He lifted her foot to his face. "What spot? These feet are so tiny."

She giggled again. His attempt at a foot massage had started well, but had turned into a tickle Tally session. She laid on the sofa, her torso on Connor's lap and her feet on Theron.

"My feet are not tiny. You better stop saying that."

"They really are," Connor agreed, brushing curls away from her face.

"Are you two blind? Didn't you see how swollen they are?" She glanced into Connor's laughing eyes.

"You decided to dance the night away."

She groaned. "I know, but how could I dance so much with you and then not with Theron?"

Theron snorted. "I was more than happy to watch you dance. I told you that."

She shook her head, watching him rub circles over her ankles. "I felt guilty. I want you both to feel my time is spread evenly with you."

"Tally, we don't suffer from insecurities. We're united, not competing," Theron replied.

If only she could remember that. Most of the time she was too worried about not making one feel less wanted than the other that she sometimes overdid it.

"I had fun tonight," she said. Thinking back to all the family events of the past, none came close to her cousin's wedding.

"Your grandmother sure laid it out there for Paul," Connor snickered.

"Oh my god, did you hear her tell him she'd shove her cane up his ass? If I hadn't been so angry I would've burst into giggles."

"You know, she was right," Theron said, meeting her gaze with a smile. "You're not alone. You've got us, too."

She wanted to open up and say something emotional, but held back. She'd been analyzing her feeling and had come to the conclusion there was something deeper there between the three of them. Something she couldn't name yet, but that she was willing to spend more time developing.

"Thank you, I appreciate that."

CHAPTER EIGHT

"So remind me again, why having two men any woman would kill for that want you is a bad thing?" Nita smiled at the waitress that brought their coffee and cake.

"I'm not saying it's a bad thing for them to want me," Tally grumbled.

Maybe. Okay, she didn't think it was bad they wanted her. Hell, it was like her deepest wet dream come true. Two super-hot guys who wanted her, spent time making sure she not only saw their interest, but felt wanted.

"So why the long face?" Nita put her usual too much sugar and cream and sipped her coffee.

"Because of my history, Nita. I have bad luck with men. And these guys are so..."

Wonderful. She didn't want to say it, but for the past few weeks, she'd either gone to dinner, movies, walks and shows with one the other or both. And the sex? The best, porn had nothing on them. They were the best team out there. One focused on a particular part of her while the other worked another until she was begging one or both to fuck her. Heat crowded her cheeks. She'd lost every last scrap of inhibition and had let loose the sex drive she had no idea lived inside her.

"So what?" Nita asked, bringing her back to the present.

"So damn nice! They deserve a good woman who will make them a good mate. Not some inse-cure, bitter, fat girl that man-hates and wants to tie them in the closet so nobody else gets their claws on them," she said honestly.

"First of all, you are not a fat girl. You have curves. And so the fuck what if you are fat, I am too and let me tell you, we fucking rock."

"I know that. I am not saying we don't. Until I met these two, I never felt self-conscious of my body. I'm pretty happy with myself. I know I won't be a skinny woman. I know I can't fit into the sizes most women wear and that's okay. I am fine with that. What I am having a problem with is the fact that they bring out my insecurities."

She eyed the cake on her plate. If only it would solve all the problems in her life. There was no real answer to things other than taking chances. She didn't like the idea of making a decision she'd later regret. She was at a point in life where she felt she'd wasted all the time she was going to waste in a useless relationship.

"Let me ask you a few questions," Nita said. "How do you feel when you are with Connor?"

She smiled. "He's such a sweetheart. So worried about my feelings all the time. He has this...something that he knows when I'm feeling worried or sad and he'll hug me without saying a word."

Connor's actions had really broken through a lot of barriers in her. She tried, but it was useless to keep him at a distance. His constant care and concern for her proved to her that he was genuine in his feelings.

"I think one of the biggest parts of all this is that he is so scared about me meeting their pack." She bit down on a piece of heavenly chocolate cake.

Whenever they spoke of her meeting the

pack, Connor would frown or hold her tighter as if hoping to protect her from the people she'd have to one day meet if she took them up on their offer.

"What about Theron?" Nita pressed. "How do you feel with him?"

Oh, lord of all naughty things. Theron had the sex drive of her dream man. He was rougher, tougher and wilder in bed. He wanted to do things to her she'd never even thought of. While Connor was the sweeter side of the man of her dreams, Theron was the rugged, panty-tearing biker that could fuck her raw and leave her shaking in the aftermath.

Together they made up the perfect man. Her perfect combo. But time was running out and she'd have to tell them soon if she was willing to be their mate or if they would need to continue their search for someone else.

"Tally?"

"Theron is amazing in bed. He has a fantastic sense of humor and if I could bottle the two of them up we'd have the recipe for the man every woman dreams of."

Nita slammed her cup down on the saucer. "I

still don't understand what the hell your problem is!"

Tally watched her cousin glare at her for the first time in years. "What the heck, Nita?"

"No, you listen. You have two men you've described as every woman's dream, licking at your heels and ready to do your bidding. Men offering you protection, love, devotion and a relationship neither would ever do anything to damage and you still can't decide?"

She bit her lip and glanced away. Nita was right. What the hell was wrong with her? When would she ever meet two men as willing and ready to make her their life? Not anytime soon if ever.

"You're right. I'm such an idiot."

Nita grinned. "You're not an idiot. You're scared to try something new. But there's something you seem to have forgotten in your search for everything wrong with these two guys."

"What?"

"You're already in a relationship with them or they wouldn't be practically living in your house. You sleep with both of them. You have sex with both of them. Hell, you shower with one and then the other." She sniggered. "I bet you'd do both in the shower if your shower wasn't so damn small."

She flushed and glanced around. "Hey, just because I am ready to give the whole mate thing a chance doesn't mean I want the entire world in on my sex life."

"Fine, but you really need to give those men the mate they desperately need." Nita patted her hand. "They've been patient with you for almost two weeks. They need you to make a move already." Nita stared deep in her eyes. "You are not a punk, prima. You're a self-assured woman who knows what is good and what isn't. Is this good for you? Do these men make you happy? Only you know the answer to that."

She thought about Nita's questions for the rest of the day. She was right. Tally had become a good judge of what was good for her life. She knew that Connor and Theron had taken more than just an interest in all the things that made her happy. They'd turned the entire situation into a way for her to see that a relationship between the three could work. Neither man pushed or pulled for more of her attention than she wanted to give.

They were so concerned with what she wanted that she was shocked at how much they paid attention. It caught her off guard one night when Connor showed up with a tub of her favorite ice cream. He said she'd been running low. It was her favorite when they watched TV at night. For him to notice that was beyond what she'd ever expected out of anyone.

Even Theron, the big sexual wolf had found ways to make her feel cared for when she wasn't aware of it. He'd given her hugs and kisses when they sat down doing simple things like talk. Whenever they walked anywhere, he always held her hand. It was all those little things that added to the bigger thing she'd tried to deny. Her obvious feelings for them.

Denying it wouldn't make it go away. They cared and dammit she did too. It was time to stop with the games and come out with what she knew they needed. Her answer on being their mate. They hadn't mentioned it again except the few times they spoke of her going to meet their pack. But she knew that they waited anxiously for her to make up her mind.

That evening, she got home and found dinner on the table, candles lit and wine chilling. Theron sat on the sofa watching a game while Connor read a newspaper.

She stopped at the sight of both men. Her

stomach flipped when they smiled. Her heart filled with an emotion she didn't want to define just yet.

"We need to talk," she burst out.

Their smiles dimmed. They glanced at each other and back at her.

"Tally, if anything's wrong—" Connor started.

She raised a hand and cut him off. "Stop, please. I need to talk. You both need to listen."

They nodded but remained silent. She put her handbag on a chair and slipped off her heels. To help herself relax, she curled her toes into the soft beige carpet and sighed. If nothing else, the soft-ness allowed her to take a mental breather and focus on what she wanted to say.

"Okay, so you both said you wanted to have this mating relationship with me, right?"

Dual nods again.

"And you both promised to be faithful and not look for another woman while we're together," she said, saying their words back to them. "I've made a decision. I don't know how or why you two decided I was the woman for you." She watched both, loving Theron's fierce concentra-tion on dissecting everything she said and Connor's encouraging smile. "I'll be your mate."

She cleared her throat. "That is, if you still want me."

Both men jumped to their feet.

"Of course we want you!" Theron growled.

"You are the only woman we want," Connor added.

She shifted from foot to foot, unsure what to do. Connor nodded at Theron, who marched toward her, the bright glow of his animal clear for her to see. He swept her into his arms and carried her to the bedroom.

"What are you doing?" She gasped, throwing her hands around his neck to hold on.

"We're about to make you our mate." He rubbed his face on her cheek.

"Now?" she squeaked. She hadn't expected it would happen right away. She thought there was some kind of...ritual or something that needed to happen. Like when one got married. Only shifter style. Went to show she really needed to ask more questions about their kind.

Connor followed directly behind them. He removed his clothes, dropping all articles on his walk to the bedroom. She bit her lip at the sight of his strong sexy body. He didn't have all the tattoos that Theron had. Instead, his body was pure muscled perfection. Hairless and smooth, she could lick him for hours and not need a break.

She glanced down at his fully erect cock. Her mouth watered. Damn she loved touching his body. Having him touch her. Hell, having both of them touch her was the highlight of her day. On days they both treated her like she was some kind of goddess, she went to sleep with a smile on her face. Most days, she woke up that way too.

Theron dropped her on the bed. She landed on the soft blankets with her legs spread open. Modesty had gone out the window. Connor searched through her nightstand drawer for something while Theron stripped. He was also fully aroused and so big and ready she bit her lip to keep from moaning.

"Come here," Theron ordered. His facial lines tightened but remained human. As though his animal wanted control.

She crawled toward him on the bed. When she reached the edge, he glanced at her lips, his eyes bright gold. "Are you very attached to this dress?"

She blinked. Christ that deep rough voice set her blood on fire. "Not really."

"Good." He caressed her cheek and slid his

hand down her front so softly she was caught off guard by the low sound of tearing fabric.

She peeked down to see the front of her dress split open. Theron grabbed the material and slid it off her body so carefully, she almost didn't believe he'd been the one to tear it. Her bra and panties suffered the same fate. The articles of clothing were discarded and soon she was kneeling naked on the bed.

Connor came around the bed with a bottle of lube. She gulped, her hormones went into a frenzy. Theron slipped a hand into her hair and tugged her forward. He kissed her hard. Their lips and tongues melded and clashed. A struggle for dominance ensued. She no longer worried about being shy with either man. She'd allowed her inner demanding woman to come out. She took what she wanted from them. Her feelings for them had allowed her to open the door to trusting that they'd meet her needs both in and out of bed. And now she couldn't get enough of them.

Theron cupped her heavy breasts. He molded and squeezed her sensitive flesh in his calloused hands. She moaned into the kiss. He pinched her nipples, tweaking and fondling her. The hard tugs sent electrical shards straight to her clit. She was wet, throbbing. Her body burned for her two men.

He pushed her tits together and broke their kiss.

"You know I love sucking your nipples. You have beautiful tits and I love the faces you make when I suck them."

She inhaled sharply, her brain a complete mess. Her skin felt on fire. The urgent need to have them both inside her hit her so hard she lost her breath. That's what would make her whole. Both men taking her. Owning her. Making her theirs.

"Lie back, gorgeous." Theron crawled on the bed at the same time she leaned back on the pillows. She spread her legs fast. His look of pure hunger and possession only added gasoline to the raging fire inside her core.

He curled large arms around her big thighs and inhaled. "So fucking sweet. Every time I taste you it's like eating ripe berries."

Her mouth lost all moisture. Her tongue stuck to the roof of her mouth. Connor came around the bed, his eyes also glowed a bright gold.

She gasped. Theron's lips brushed her clit at the same moment Connor leaned down and kissed her. Their kiss started off light. A mere sweep of his lips over hers. Theron's tongue flicked hard from her ass up to her slit. She groaned into Connor's mouth. The sensation of Theron's thick tongue fucking her pussy sent a fresh wave of cream down her channel.

He rumbled. She slipped one hand into his hair and gripped a chunk, while she slid the other hand between Connor's legs and found his cock. She jerked him in her grasp. Her tight hold and jerk had him moaning in no time.

Theron growled while rubbing his tongue on her pussy. He licked up and down her slick folds. Up to her clit and down to her hole. Over and over. She sucked on Connor's tongue, wishing she was sucking his cock, but her brain couldn't think past the wonderful sensation of Theron's eating her pussy like he was starved and she was his final meal.

She jerked Connor, felt the wetness dripping over her hand and used his pre-cum to coat him and continue jerking. Connor pinched her nipples. She was oh so sensitive when it came to having her breasts squeezed, tweaked or fondled.

She pulled away from Connor's mouth to gasp. "Oh, my..."

Connor wouldn't be deterred. He consumed her lips once again in a hard kiss that drove his tongue deep into her mouth. He rubbed and twined his mouth over hers like a snake doing a mating dance.

Theron flicked his tongue over her clit in a quick rotation. He didn't stop. Not when she started shaking or taking hollow breaths in her kiss with Connor. Not when Connor pinched harder and she became lost in the sensations of both men playing her body like a musical instrument.

Connor licked a wet trail from her lips to her chest. He sucked one of her nipples deep into his mouth and bit down on her breast. She moaned as he did the same thing back and forth to both nipples.

Theron moved his tongue faster. His sucks turned rougher. Finally he sucked her clit into his mouth and grazed his teeth over the throbbing nerve bundle. She gasped. Choked. Both men bit down and she screamed. Tension snapped inside her as a wave of pleasure blasted from her pussy out to her limbs. She felt weightless. As if all her bones had liquefied and she couldn't even get her lungs to work.

Connor lifted her into his arms. She was still trying to take a breath when he sat down at the edge of the bed and put her in position to straddle him. She gripped his shoulders and placed a thigh to either side of him then slid down. He held his cock as she lowered to his lap. He slid his shaft back and forth, using her juices for lubrication. A breath later, he was pulling her hips down, urging her to take his dick into her slick sex.

"Oh!" She loved the feel of him stretching her pussy and rubbing her insides. She immediately started to ride him, her body ready and wet, looking for another release not too far away.

Connor leaned back, he pulled her down with him. Then Theron was there, his hand caressing the curve of her ass down to her hole.

"Do you know how we're going to claim you?" he asked.

She shook her head, a hot shudder shot down her spine.

Theron pressed his lips on the back of her right shoulder. "We're going to fuck you at the same time. Connor will be in your pussy." He groaned. "I do love your pussy. But today I get your sweet sexy backside." He grabbed handful of her large cheeks and squeezed hard. "I get to slide my cock into this tiny hole and feel you grip me tight." He licked down her spine. "Then I get to come in your ass at the same time he comes in your pussy." His voice turned deeper. Rough. "And do you know what happens after that?"

She moaned and swallowed hard. "No."

CHAPTER NINE

Connor continued to urge her to ride him. She loved his cock inside her. But to have them both. That was something they had yet to do. Something she'd been dying to try but hadn't suggested for fear they would reject the idea.

"After that, I get to fuck your pussy and he gets to fuck your ass and we get to do you all over again," Theron rumbled. "Until we've both had you and filled you with our seed. We'll both bite you and then you'll be ours. Nobody else could ever claim you because you will wear our scents. Our marks. You'll be ours fully."

She almost came listening to his words.

Connor slid his hands up to cup her breasts and thumb her nipples.

"You are so sexy, Tally," he said softly. "Your body is gorgeous and I love being inside you."

She didn't get a chance to say anything, not that she could. Theron dropped a trail of lube down the crack of her ass. Then he worked the lube into her with one finger. She wiggled on Connor's hard cock, wanting to ride him but at the same time waited to see what else Theron would do. He added a second finger, the burning of her anal muscles increased.

"Don't tense, sweetheart," Theron whispered, pushing his fingers in and out of her. At first slow and then with increased speed and frequency. "That's right, let your muscles relax. Take my fingers."

He plunged them deep into her hole. In. Out. Then he added a third finger, the burning and stretching a lot more intense than before.

Connor attached his lips to her tit and he sucked hard. She jerked on his lap. Her pussy squeezed at his dick as she tried to pay attention to his pulsing cock and Theron's fingers. She pushed back, wanting Theron to continue the thrusting of his fingers once she got over the burning discomfort.

He pulled out and Connor moved to her other breast. He sucked her all over. Hard. Rough. So unlike him and it felt so good. She forgot all about Theron until he pushed the head of his greased up cock into her asshole. The burning started again, but not as much as before.

"Fuck," he groaned, his breath right by her ear. "You're so tight. I can hardly get in there. Relax those muscles and let me in, baby."

She pushed back. The move rocked Connor's dick in her pussy and she moaned at the sensation. Theron pressed into her ass. He slowly drove himself into her. Before she knew it, he was in her. Both men deep inside and pulsing hard.

"Jesus. Someone move or I'm going to die," she groaned.

Theron pulled back until he was almost fully out and then pushed all the way in. Not hard, but not as softly as before. She rocked on Connor's dick. Then both men took control. Connor held her up and lifted his hips to thrust into her at the same time Theron pulled back. When Theron drove into her, Connor pulled back. Both men worked with amazing speed and rhythm. She clawed at Connor's arms.

"Oh my God. Oh my God. Oh my God!" She couldn't seem to catch a breath.

Her ass and pussy clenched in tandem with both thrusts and retreats. She'd never felt anything like it. The sizzle in her womb turned into an electric spark that lit every cell in her body. She moaned. There were no words to describe how amazing it felt to be taken by both the men she wanted at the same time. A new emotion unlocked in her heart.

Theron licked the back of her right shoulder. He thrust deeper, harder. Every drive pulled a new moan out of her. Connor swept his tongue over the front of her right shoulder. Both men fucked and licked her at the same time. She could not for the life of her form a coherent sentence or thought.

Connor slipped a hand between her slick pussy lips. Right where her hard little clit peeked from its hood.

"Come on, Tally," Theron groaned on her back. "Let go, baby."

Connor thumbed the tiny bundle, slow at first and then harder. Rougher. Until she could do no more than feel the tension snap and her body shake from the almost painful orgasm that overtook her. Waves of bliss rocked her from head to toe. Theron and Connor both growled and bit down on her at the same time. She moaned. The painful bites sent her over the edge so fast she choked on the air rushing into her lungs.

Their movements turned jerky, until they stopped altogether and at first Theron growled into her back. Then Connor did the same, his teeth still biting into her front. Both men came in her then. Hot. Deep. For long moments their cocks pulsed and jetted warm semen into her ass and pussy. She couldn't have moved if she wanted to. She was held up by Theron's arm around her waist.

They fell on to their sides on the bed. Connor pulled out of her body first, then Theron slowly followed. His wet cock nestled right between her cheeks. She moaned as they both caressed her breasts, down to her waist and rained kisses all over her. From her neck to shoulders, they kissed everywhere they reached. Theron slid his hand down her side, to her breasts and fondled a nipple. Connor roamed a hand around her hip to grab a handful of her hips.

"You're ours now," Theron murmured. "There's no one else for you or us."

She sighed. She knew that already. She hadn't made the decision lightly. They might not be what she considered the traditional couple, but she'd never had luck with a traditional anything. This was a new step in her life and she had to do whatever made her happy.

Theron and Connor made her happy.

"I want inside your pussy." Theron kissed behind her ear. Goosebumps broke over her arms.

"You do?" She moaned and flipped over to face him.

He grinned, his bright golden eyes those of a predator. "Oh, baby. I always want inside your tight pussy."

"And it's my turn in your ass," Connor rumbled behind her. He slid a finger between her cheeks and into her hole. Her anal muscles sucked it right in. "Fuck that is awesome."

"I think a shower is in order first," she mumbled.

"No," they said in unison.

"Our mating process isn't over until we've both had you. Every way possible." Theron licked his lips. "Once we have, then you can have all the warm baths you want. Until then…" He pulled her head toward his and kissed her. "We fuck."

Though she wasn't used to the animalistic tones and the need for dirty sex, she definitely enjoyed having Theron and Connor inside her at the same time. That was something she'd easily grow used to.

"Fine. Fuck me. Both of you. But then you better feed me."

"TODAY WE GO VISIT OUR PACK," Theron declared just two days after their mating.

"Are you sure? I mean, I thought you guys were all worried about me being around your pack women," she grumbled. She didn't like that they took turns going back and forth to deal with the Wildwoods Pack and she was often left without one of them. Though it gave her alone time with the other mate, she would like the time to be because they wanted it that way, not because they were afraid to bring her around their people.

"They'll get used to you. Or deal with me."

"What if they don't like me?" she muttered.

"Then I'll handle them."

She shook her head with a grin. "You can't fix everything for me, Theron. I have to be able to handle your pack too if they're going to be a part of my life."

"Yes, but that's what I'm there for. I'm the alpha. You're my mate. And I won't let anyone disrespect you."

"I'm more worried about you not letting me out of your sight until you've had your way with me again."

He gave her a hot look. "You have gotten to know me so well. You've gotten used to my kind of sex."

She had and boy did she love it.

"You mean the all day, every day kind?" She was still getting used to the aches from the longest night of sex ever. She'd enjoyed it, but damn had she been fucked raw. Of course, just thinking about it made her instantly wet.

"I like that smell," he said with devilish grin.

"Oh, cut it out. You do this to me every single time you look at me," she grumbled.

He sat down on the armrest of the sofa and pulled her between his legs. "I want you to always have that need for me. For us. I want you to get wet when we look at you. When anything reminds you of us. You are ours and that means we want you to want to be with us. All the time."

She sniffed. "That doesn't help me when I have to go to work, you know."

He chuckled and hugged her. She curled her arms around his neck and leaned into him.

"I know it doesn't, but you decided you wanted to continue working. We've given you the option to stop."

She shook her head. "No way am I depending on you two for money for the rest of my life. I'm an independent woman. I pay my own way in life."

He slid his hands down her back and pressed her ass forward until her pussy was flush with his erection.

"Oh, Theron, stop..."

"I won't. You are my mate and I want to fuck you every hour of every day. You have a body that makes me so hard I can't think straight."

She gave up. Heck who was she kidding? She wanted him to fuck her too. She walked back and tugged the dress over her head. He was so easy. He growled and she giggled. "Connor will be sad he missed this."

"He can have alone time with you later." Theron grinned.

That was the amazing thing about them. They both knew she needed to spend alone time with each so their individual relationships could deepen. It was what made the entire mating that much more special. She glanced down and before she knew it he threw her over his shoulder and ran for the bedroom.

"Theron!"

"You walk too slow, baby. I want to fuck now!"

She laughed as she landed on the sheets in a tangle. She didn't get a chance to fix herself when he was on her, his hands held either side of her head.

"I love you, Tally."

She gasped, her heart beat painfully loud in her ears. "Are you sure? It's so soon."

He nodded. "I don't want to hear you say the words if or until you ever feel the emotion. But I wanted you to know. You've seeped into my pores, sunk into my blood and made me an addict. I can't be without you. I don't want to be."

She blinked back tears. She didn't think Theron had those kinds of words in him. "I don't know what to say."

"Don't say anything, love." He pressed a kiss over her lips. "You're here. That's all I need."

She nodded and kissed him back. The relationship between them grew another string at that moment to make their link that much stronger. When he made love to her that day, she felt it in the deepest areas of her heart. Those areas she'd thought untouched until then.

CHAPTER TEN

T ally bit her lip. Nerves sucked. But she
didn't know how to stop herself from
showing them. Theron led her into a
community of houses in a forested area. It was
growing late in the day. The sun's light had
dimmed through the thick trees. She'd swear it
was closer to nighttime than early evening.

"Theron..."

"Relax, darling. You shouldn't be afraid," he
admonished.

"I'm not afraid." She truly wasn't. She was
nervous. Meeting people had a bad effect on her.
She tended to be sarcastic and a lot of times
nerves made her babble. "I'm a little weirded out
about meeting new people is all."

"Don't worry, love. We'll both be here for you."

Lovely. The fact both her men, which happened to be the leaders of this pack, were there as her babysitters didn't really give her any warm fuzzies.

"Where's Connor?" she asked just as they reached an open area where a large group gathered at the center. She stopped dead in her tracks.

There were a lot of glowing gold eyes staring at her. Instinct told her to move back. To get away from the danger, but something new and angry roared to life inside her. An emotion she'd never known she possessed spread wings and took hold of every one of her cells. Dominance.

She squared her shoulders and continued forward. No longer worried about what the people might think, now she worried about what Connor and Theron would think of her.

"Thank you all for coming tonight," Connor greeted the large group. His voice was low, so she didn't know how she could hear him so far away.

"We want to meet your new third," a woman said. She was tall. Much taller and slimmer than Tally. With beautiful porcelain skin and rich auburn hair. The woman didn't smile. She eyed

Tally with open interest. "My name is Aura. What is yours?"

Tally opened her mouth but Theron answered for her.

"Her name is Talia or Tally," Theron said to Aura.

Another woman, circled by three others, moved forward. She had chocolate-brown skin and short curly hair. Almond-shaped eyes glared at Tally. "She doesn't look to be Alpha mate material."

Theron growled low. Tally almost got whiplash glancing to the side to see his partially shifted face and looming stance. "You have a problem with our choice of mate, Keya?"

The woman, Keya, continue to stare at Tally with hostility. Her eyes brightened with her animal. "Maybe. You know the rules, Theron." Keya took a step forward. The other women hovered behind her. "She can be challenged."

"Why would she be?" Theron growled. "She's our choice. It is not up for debate."

Tally's insides burned with anger. She'd never been a people person, but Keya's death-glares were making it hard for her to want to like her. Fury bubbled in her blood, growing heated and explosive with every word thrown back and forth between Theron and Keya. Her muscles burned. She blinked the group into focus, but it was hard. Her vision swam every few seconds. It was like having her pupils dilate and try to focus once again.

"She looks like a weakling," Keya spat. She took another handful of steps until she stood in the center of the clearing. People moved back to give her space. The crowd was quiet.

Tally glanced at the spot where Connor stood. She cocked her head to make out what his features tried to tell her. Then, she heard it. A distant calling to her in her mind.

"What exactly do you want, Keya? You were not a choice for us at any point." Theron's voice sounded like it was coming from under water.

"I demand a challenge for the Alpha third spot. Now," she said, her voice deep with her coming shift.

"Talia is not ready for a challenge," Theron argued.

"Too bad. You are Alpha. You know our rules. She accepts or she leaves and her position is mine," Keya said.

Theron growled next to Tally. She'd swear she

could understand his growl which was absolute insanity.

Then she heard the calling in her brain again. She marched to the woman, ignoring Theron, and stopped in front of her.

"They don't want you. Don't you understand English?"

The shifter smirked and Tally's new and unusual anger flew off the handle. She slapped the other woman hard. So fast she almost wouldn't believe it had it not been for the shocked gasp that sounded around them.

"You are so dead." Keya growled and swiped a shifting claw across Tally's arm.

Fire spread across her shoulder and blood oozed down to her elbow.

"Enough!" Theron's voice thundered.

"Let them fight, Theron," Connor ordered. "You know our rules. We cannot break them for anyone. Especially our own mate. She will be fine."

Tally almost smiled at the amount of conviction in Connor's voice. She could hardly see one step ahead of her and her insides felt like they were going up in flames.

The burning in her limbs increased. Keya

pushed her hard. She stumbled back and lost her footing. She twisted her body at the last second and landed on all fours.

"Look at her. How could you want her when she cannot even defend herself in her human body? Do you think she will survive my wolf?" Keya's voice grew so rough it was impossible to make out her words. "We shall see now."

Tally forgot all about Keya and her animal. She focused on the pain and spreading fire taking over her muscles.

"What is she doing?" someone asked.

"She's in pain," she heard Aura say. "She needs help. She is our new Alpha."

"No interfering," Connor commanded. "Tally will be fine."

Tally wanted to yell at him to shut the fuck up and help her. If only she could figure out what was wrong. She'd lost control of her body. Muscles shook and burned. The sound of something breaking came from so close she worried Keya had attacked her and she was too far gone to notice. Of all the people, the last person she'd think would allow her to be in pain was Connor. That big jerk.

She grabbed hold of her anger and let it grow.

It expanded. Something tickled under her skin, pushing out. Then a large growl tore from her throat.

"She's—"

"Shifted," Theron said with pride.

The fact she was on all fours and in a wolf body would have to wait to be dissected at another time. Keya's large brown wolf charged to Tally. Keya was fast. She zoomed right for her, canines on full display. But Tally wouldn't let anyone, man or woman, abuse her in any form. Fuck that.

She waited until the last second, jumped to the right and turned, kicking Keya's wolf with her brand new hind legs. She kicked as hard as she could and it seemed to work. When she turned, she saw Keya's animal sliding on the dusty clearing.

"You think you can beat me?" Keya spoke through some kind of animal link.

"I am not trying to beat you. You're the one that doesn't know how to understand that Connor and Theron don't want you. Why don't you stop? It doesn't have to be this way." She tried to reason with the other woman.

"No." She growled and made a leap for Tally

again. This time she managed to dig a claw right into Tally's side.

"*Fuck!*" Pain shot all down her side, igniting the fury that pushed for her change.

The wolf within wanted to be in control. There was no other way. Tally allowed the beast free rein.

It was like watching a movie. She was doing things but no longer in control. The wolf in Tally was angry, hurting and not willing to give Keya another chance to back down. She didn't try to push off the other wolf. She went right for her. Keya appeared shocked and was caught off guard when Tally clawed at her muzzle and snatched up one of her paws in her mouth. She crunched down, breaking something in the process.

Keya scratched back. She kicked and fought to push Tally off. Her angry efforts served for Tally to release the paw and dig her claws into Keya's side. Tally bit down on Keya's tail and yanked her back.

Keya howled in pain. Another round of gasps went around the clearing. Tally's animal was bent on revenge. She eyed the other wolf as Keya tried to turn with a broken leg. Tally jumped on her back and bit down on the neck area her animal knew to go for. Keya was no longer in control. The tighter Tally squeezed her jaw on Keya's neck, the louder Keya howled.

Death and killing was not in her. She might be a bitch, bitter and angry, but she wasn't ready to take anyone's life.

"Let her go, Tally," Theron whispered softly in her mind.

"You don't have to do anything that you don't want to," Connor added.

Tally released the injured wolf and took steps back until she stood between both Theron and Connor. The wolf inside her retreated at that point and her body took control once again. Limbs shifted. Connor and Theron helped her stand in front of the crowd.

Connor wrapped a blanket over her shoulders. "Sorry about your clothes, love. But it happens when you shift. You tear through things."

She nodded. Her throat was dry and she needed a bath. A nice long hot one.

"This is our third," Theron said, his voice steely. "The next person who wants to challenge her will deal with me directly."

Aura stepped forward. "There is no need for any challenges. We have not seen a human take to the wolf so quickly and aggressively. Clearly she is the right one to help you lead."

Tally cleared her throat. Keya was dragged from the site, still in her wolf body. Tally hadn't thought someone would dislike her just because she hadn't shown enough aggression. In her human life, she'd always been told she was too aggressive and bossy. Her life had changed to something so different she didn't know if she would ever understand it fully.

The crowd glanced at her and her men. Then they tore through their clothes and shifted. The large number of wolves would have scared her at any other moment, but instead, made her curious.

"What are they doing?" she asked.

The wolves huddled close and one by one lowered their muzzles to her feet. When they were all done, they scampered into the woods.

"They were showing you their loyalty. For a wolf to lower its head, they have to feel you are the stronger party. You're their Alpha now."

It took her a moment to realize the extent of his words. She shook her head and decided she had way too much to adjust to before she thought about that.

"Show me to a shower." She wrinkled her nose. "I ache and stink."

"You got it, beautiful. After that performance you deserve anything you want." Connor winked.

"Look at you, all blood thirsty. Who would've thought you had it in you." She laughed.

TALLY SAT BACK on the picnic blanket and watched the sunset over the horizon. Theron lay to one side of her and Connor to the other. For the past few weeks, they'd given her exactly what she'd asked for and all they'd wanted was her. Nothing but her. It was time.

"I love you," she said, still glancing at the setting sun.

They sat up so fast she bit back a giggle.

"Who? Who do you love?" Theron asked.

"Tell us, please," Connor's plea tore at her heart. She shouldn't have made them wait so long. They had embraced her as their woman from the very first day and she'd been too afraid to give in and take what they offered freely.

"Both of you." She glanced at Theron and brushed her lips over his. "I love you, Theron.

You and your quirky sense of humor and amazing oral skills."

"I love you, Tally." He kissed her.

She turned to face Connor. "I love you, Connor. Your ability to look deep into my heart and help me see a side of me I never knew existed is priceless. Your care and concern over my feelings is unmatched."

"I love you, beautiful Tally," Connor murmured and kissed her softly.

"You both have given me what I never realized I wanted. Two men to make me whole."

They leaned in, Theron cupping her face to kiss her mouth and Connor sliding his hands under her tank top. She'd always joked that a woman needed two men to make her happy. In her case, that was the absolute truth. Two amazing, growly, possessive men to bring out the Alpha wolf in her.

"I just wanted to thank you again," Tally smiled.

Gerri couldn't have been more pleased. Something had told her that Tally would be perfect with Theron and Connor. Her instinct never guided her wrong.

"You're very welcome my dear. I only want to see you all happy," she said honestly.

Tally grinned at the men to either side of her. "We are. We're very happy. And I owe it all to you."

"Thanks Aunt Gerri," Theron said. "We'll see you next week for dinner."

She waved them away with a smile. A moment later her cell phone rang.

"Paranormal Dating Agency, how can I help you?" Gerri answered her business cell phone with a smile.

"Hi, is this Mrs. Wilder?" A woman asked hesitantly.

"Yes, it is. Who might you be?" She glanced at the open file on her desk. An unruly bear shifter who didn't want a mate but his sister was adamant he get one. The name his sister provided for the mate was a much more difficult task. A human. One she'd recently become familiar with through her neighbor.

"This is Nita, Tally's cousin. She gave me your card and said you could um...that I could use your services."

Gerri grinned. Would wonders never cease? It was perfect. A plan formed in her mind. "She told me about you, Nita. Said you were a no-nonsense type of woman."

Nita laughed softly. "Yeah, that's me. So, I am interested in seeing who you can match me up with."

"I think I can help you." Gerri picked up the address to her unsuspecting bear client. "Tell me something, do you like mountain getaways?"

"I do, but I was looking for a possible date."

Gerri picked up a pen and wrote down notes. "This definitely is a date. You'll have to travel a bit since my client is out of the city, but I know he'll just love meeting someone just as no-nonsense as him."

"Oh, wonderful! I'm more than happy to try."

"Excellent. Come by and see me. I have everything you need."

Gerri hung up with a smile. That bear had no idea what was coming. Then again, neither did the human. This would be fun.

CONTINUE the series with Geek Bearing Gifts

THE END

ABOUT THE AUTHOR

New York Times and USA Today Bestselling Author

Hi! I'm Milly Taiden. I love to write sexy stories featuring fun, sassy heroines with curves and growly alpha males with fur. My books are a great way to satisfy your craving for paranormal romance with action, humor, suspense and happily ever afters.

I live in Florida with my hubby, our kids, and our fur babies: Speedy, Stormy and Teddy. I have a serious addiction to chocolate and cake.

I love to meet new readers, so come sign up for my newsletter and check out my Facebook page. We always have lots of fun stuff going on there.

SIGN UP FOR MILLY'S NEWSLETTER FOR
LATEST NEWS!
   http://eepurl.com/pt9q1

Find out more about Milly here:
www.millytaiden.com
milly@millytaiden.com

Find out more about Milly Taiden here:

Email: millytaiden@gmail.com

Website: http://www.millytaiden.com

Facebook: http://www.facebook.com/millytaidenpage

Twitter: https://www.twitter.com/millytaiden

Nightflame Dragons

Dragons' Jewel *Book One*

Dragons' Savior *Book Two*

Dragons' Bounty *Book Three*

Dragon's Prize *Book Four*

A.L.F.A Series

Elemental Mating *Book One*

Mating Needs *Book Two*

Dangerous Mating *Book Three*

Fearless Mating *Book Four*

Savage Shifters

Savage Bite *Book One*

Savage Kiss *Book Two*

Savage Hunger *Book Three*

Sci-Fi - Guardian Warriors

The Alien Warrior's Woman *Book One*

The Alien's Rebel *Book Two*

Drachen Mates

Bound in Flames *Book One*

Bound in Darkness *Book Two*

Bound in Eternity *Book Three*

Bound in Ashes *Book Four*

Federal Paranormal Unit

Wolf Protector *Federal Paranormal Unit Book One*

Dangerous Protector *Federal Paranormal Unit Book Two*

Unwanted Protector *Federal Paranormal Unit Book Three*

Deadly Protector *Federal Paranormal Unit Book Four*

Alpha Geek

Alpha Geek: *Knox*

Alpha Geek: *Zeke*

Paranormal Dating Agency

Twice the Growl *Book One*

Geek Bearing Gifts *Book Two*

The Purrfect Match *Book Three*

Curves 'Em Right *Book Four*

Tall, Dark and Panther *Book Five*

The Alion King *Book Six*

There's Snow Escape *Book Seven*

Scaling Her Dragon *Book Eight*

In the Roar *Book Nine*

Scrooge Me Hard *Short One*

Bearfoot and Pregnant *Book Ten*

All Kitten Aside *Book Eleven*

Oh My Roared *Book Twelve*

Piece of Tail *Book Thirteen*

Kiss My Asteroid *Book Fourteen*

Scrooge Me Again *Short Two*

Born with a Silver Moon *Book Fifteen*

Sun in the Oven *Book Sixteen*

Between Ice and Frost *Book Seventeen*

Scrooge Me Again *Book Eighteen*

Winter Takes All *Book Nineteen*

You're Lion to Me *Book Twenty*

Lion on the Job *Book Twenty-One*

Beasts of Both Worlds *Book Twenty-Two*

Also, check out the **Paranormal Dating Agency World on Amazon**

Or visit http://mtworldspress.com

The Alien Warrior's Woman *Book One*

The Alien's Rebel *Book Two*

Contemporary Works

Mr. Buff

Stranded Temptation

Lucky Chase

Their Second Chance

Club Duo Boxed Set

A Hero's Pride

A Hero Scarred

A Hero for Sale

Wounded Soldiers Set

If you enjoyed the book, please consider leaving a review, even if it's only a line or two; it would make all the difference and would be very much appreciated.

Thank you!

CPSIA information can be obtained
at www.ICGtesting.com
Printed in the USA
LVHW011212041119
636244LV00003B/426